King Jerry

King Jerry

a novel by

David Arnason

TURNSTONE PRESS

Turnstone Press
607-100 Arthur Street
Artspace Building
Winnipeg, MB
R3B 1H3 Canada
www.TurnstonePress.com

Turnstone Press gratefully acknowledges the assistance of
The Canada Council for the Arts, the Manitoba Arts Council
and the Government of Canada through the Book Publishing Industry
Development Program for our publishing activities.

The Canada Council | Le Conseil des Arts
for the Arts | du Canada

Canadä

Cover illustration: Hadi Farahani
Cover design: Manuela Dias
Interior design: Sharon Caseburg
Printed and bound in Canada by Friesens for Turnstone Press.

Second printing: January 2002

Canadian Cataloguing in Publication Data

Arnason, David, 1940–
 King Jerry
ISBN 0-88801-262-4
 I. Title.
PS8551.R765K5 2001   C813'.54   C2001-910814-1
PR9199.3.A558K5 2001

for Dennis

King Jerry

JERRY WAS FIFTY YEARS OLD WHEN his daughters denounced him, as he had always known they would. The oldest, Lise, was living on the coast with a pilot. She wrote to tell him that she thought his actions were unconscionable. That was the word she used. The second, Cindy, was living with a cowboy in Alberta, and she phoned one night and told him he shouldn't bother to try to get in touch with her again. The youngest, Margaret, was in residence at the University of New Brunswick. She said that she understood that he was going through some kind of crisis, and she'd help in any way she could. He said no thanks, he'd read the play, and they were all ungrateful.

It wasn't as if it was his fault. It was Thelma who'd walked out. He was still at home with the fool of a dog with the bad hip that Lise had gotten from the Humane Society when she was fifteen. And the rotten parakeet. He was going to kill the parakeet the next time it escaped from its cage and shat on the chesterfield. Thelma had discovered that she preferred women and couldn't live a lie anymore. She'd moved out and was living with her poetry-writing massage therapist in an apartment in Osgood village. Primal scream therapy had revealed to her that Jerry had beaten her when they were first married, and she had repressed it. Jerry could not remember ever having raised a hand to her other than the time she got drunk and tried to pull his pants down at a Kinsmen's picnic, and even then it had been mostly an accident. He was trying to keep his pants on, and he dropped his drink and it cut her forehead. She'd even apologized, so it must have been something else. Anyway, his daughters hated him.

He was fifty years old, an unthinkable age. An obscene age. He had a potbelly, not a big one, but, what was worse, a little one. Looking at himself sideways in the mirror, he looked exactly like the silhouette of a fifty-year-old man in a medical textbook. He wasn't bald at least. He had that. But hair had started to grow on his nose, and the barber had cheerfully trimmed the hair inside his ears the last time he'd gone for a haircut.

When he got out of the shower that morning he was certain the telephone must have rung. The air seemed to quiver with the last vibrations of the bell. He walked naked into his den, dripping water on the rug, and saw that the red light on his telephone answering machine was blinking. Thelma, he thought. Thelma with one more lunatic threat to bring action against him for cruelty. Or else one of his ungrateful daughters with a sharp moral comment.

The voice on the machine was nearly incoherent. "Umm,"

it said. "Margaret?" the voice rising in question. "I, umm, you remember, umm? Met you at the coast? Umm? Anyway. Bob gave me your number? So I was kind of hoping?" There was a long pause. "You know? So, fiveish? Okay? Oh, it's Debbie? With the long hair?" Her time ran out. It was an old machine, and it only gave callers thirty seconds. Most of them were barely into their spiels by that time. Jerry wondered what else she might have asked if she'd had time.

It was one of the affectations he hated most in women, that habit of making everything into a question. And he supposed she'd call again, and he'd have to listen to her *Umm* in person. When he backed out of the driveway, he spun a little gravel, then felt ashamed of himself. He was turning into a misanthrope. He saw that the dog had escaped and was digging in the neighbour's flower bed. Covering something. Good, he thought. Now maybe someone will call the pound and they'll come and take the stupid thing away. There'd been a letter from the vet the other day. Rover King was due for another shot. The only dog in the world actually named Rover.

At the gym, he ran five miles, did two hundred sit-ups and spent twenty-six minutes on the Nautilus machine. Then he showered and looked at himself glumly in the full-length mirror. His legs seemed to be getting skinnier, but the little potbelly resisted all the sit-ups he could do. He imagined some future, more desirable world where at fifty you could trade in your old body for a new one. A racing model, rather than the utility pick-up he was stuck with.

He supposed he should call Evelyn. Since shortly after Thelma left, he'd been seeing Evelyn in a desultory way. She had an office down the hall from him. Jerry taught in the English Department at the university, and Evelyn taught French. She was a couple of years younger than Jerry, but she had the same little potbelly. Their relationship had not become sexual, though Jerry supposed it probably would at some point. The problem was that Evelyn had what is sometimes called a self-deprecating wit. She made little jokes at her own expense, about her failing body and about the defects in her own personality. The problem was that her analysis was so devastatingly accurate that anybody else who had made it would have seemed grotesquely cruel.

No, he thought, not Evelyn. Not today. But he saw her anyway. She was picking up her mail at the very moment he came into the main office to get his. She smiled at him with her too thin lips and raised her too thin eyebrows as if in surprise. It was the way she greeted him, as if she hadn't seen him for a very long time, and was terribly surprised that he should be here, getting his mail at just this moment.

"Hello, Evelyn," he said. "How's it going?"

"Life goes on," she answered. "Day after dreary exam-ridden day."

At least she hadn't provided a French literary epithet. One day, he thought, she is going to say, "*Ou sont les neiges d'antan*," and then I will have to kill her. And that was a cruel thought, unworthy of him. Evelyn was a good friend. She would listen to him rail about the injustices of the world beyond any reasonable limit of patience, and he should try to think about her good points, not her bad.

"You've become a stranger to this place," she went on. "A ship that passes in the night."

"I'm on this exercise program," he confessed. "Trying to get into shape. It seems to take all the free time I've got, and all it has given me so far are sore knees and dry skin from all the extra showering." Which wasn't true. He had lost fifteen pounds, and was sleeping a lot better at night.

"I have news for you," Evelyn told him. "No matter how good shape you get into, you aren't going to live forever. Are you coming to the Dean's dinner tonight?"

"I'd sooner rot in hell than go to the Dean's dinner, but I suppose I'll probably do both," he said. "What time?"

"Cocktails at seven. The Club."

"Who are the other victims?"

"All the languages. English, French, German, Russian, Chinese."

"Christ. Doesn't he know anything about history? These people have been at each other's throats for centuries. Why not put English together with something innocuous like Sociology or Chemical Engineering?"

"If he thought that way, he wouldn't be a Dean, would he?"

"No, I suppose not." Jerry hated the annual Dean's dinner nearly as much as the semi-annual President's reception. Several hours of being polite to people whom you detested, and who just as cheerfully detested you.

When he got to his office Mathilde was waiting for him. She was writing her PhD dissertation on The Virgin in Canadian Literature: A Feminist-Deconstructive Approach. Or at least, she was supposed to be. In two years, she had not turned in her first chapter. She explained it would not be ready for another two weeks. She'd been ill. A yeast infection, he thought she'd said, but it couldn't be that. He must have heard incorrectly. And he didn't ask her to repeat, because he might have heard correctly.

She left just as the phone rang. Jerry let the answering machine get it. He'd only had it for a month but had come to enjoy it. He would let the caller leave a message and hurl insults at the machine as it broadcast the voice.

The phone beeped, and Thelma's voice announced itself.

"Thelma, my love," he told the machine. "Why don't you go piss up a rope?"

"Jerry, I know you're in there, you abusive pig," her voice said. "Now pick up the phone."

"Screw you, you geriatric cow," he told the machine. "I hope you die of gigantic yeast infection."

Thelma waited another second, then went on. "I've been talking to the girls. They think we should have you committed to an insane asylum. I told them I'd try to get you to go to a psychiatrist to get help."

"Your ass droops," Jerry told the machine. "It's been drooping for years, but I was always too polite to tell you."

"Now, I'm serious, Jerry. If you will agree to go for help, I think I can convince them to wait. But I have to hear from you. You can't hide behind an answering machine forever."

"You just want more money, you stupid bitch," he told the voice, which was now in the process of leaving its phone number and saying good-bye. "But you are not getting another cent."

There was a knock on the door. Ronald, the fat political scientist from next door.

"Is something wrong?"

Jerry opened the door. "No, nothing, I was cursing the phone."

"Yeah, mine's bad too. I can hardly ever get a dial tone. I know how you feel."

Jerry put a note on his door cancelling all appointments and went home. He took two Aspirins and tried to sleep. Thelma was no doubt trying to flush him out so that she could continue to torture him, but it didn't matter. If she did something insane like trying to get him committed, then he would have to defend himself, and that would be a full-time job.

He couldn't sleep, so he wandered through the house, seeing everywhere the absent female hands of his wife and daughters. Frilly curtains. Little kitschy plaques on the kitchen wall. And several closets full of female shoes and clothing. Well, if they were all gone and they weren't coming back, it was time for a house cleaning. He went from room to room gathering dresses and brassieres and shoes and stuffed animals. He gathered dozens of bottles of perfumes and unguents and powders and threw them into a cardboard box. He took everything into the back yard and began to sort it. He would call the Salvation Army in the morning, and they could pick it up.

He picked up a flowered silk dress that Thelma had worn when she sang in the choir at which she had met her new lover. On an impulse, he went to the shed, took some gasoline out of the lawn mower, and set the dress on fire. It burned in seconds with a brilliant flame that Jerry decided was beautiful. He took the rest of her clothes, dumped them in a pile and poured gasoline on them. He lit the pile on fire, and it blazed merrily.

He was debating whether to burn the rest of the clothes and risk creating grounds for his committal, when a voice behind him said, "Mmmm, are you going to like, burn all of this, mmm stuff? 'Cause if you are, I could use some of it."

Sitting on the step behind him was a very pretty young woman with long black hair. She was dressed in an old jean jacket and wearing a pair of dirty jeans with holes in the knees. She had a small plaid bag beside her, apparently her earthly possessions.

"Oh sure," Jerry said. "I was, uh, just getting this stuff ready for the Salvation Army. I burned a few things that were covered with paint. Take whatever you like."

The girl started to pick her way through the pile of clothes, holding them up and deciding that everything would fit her.

"Debbie?" he asked. "You're the girl who phoned this morning?"

"Mmmm yes," she said. "Like I met Margaret? You know? And I was like, hoping I could crash with her for a couple of days?"

"Margaret's in New Brunswick. She's at the university there." She had been there for two years, and if this girl was a friend of hers, she should have known that.

The girl sat down on the step again and burst into tears. "I've got no place to go," she said. "I've got no money. Bob dropped me off here and gave me this number. He took off with a guy named Laurie."

"And you don't know Margaret?"

"I don't know. I'm pretty sure I met her. Probably I met her if she was a friend of Bob's."

"Well, you can't stay here."

The girl started to cry again. Jerry felt that he should comfort her, but the situation was impossible.

"Take all the clothes you want," he said. He reached into his wallet. "And here's twenty bucks." She refused to look at him, and sat there crying, so he put the twenty dollars into her hand. After that he didn't know what to do, so he went back into the house and left her there. A couple of hours later, when he left for the Dean's dinner, she was still sitting on the back step.

The Dean's dinner was as bad as he had expected. Dick Thompson from the President's Office was there. He had cut the supplies budget again, and he wanted to explain the university's position. There was no photocopying budget, but individual departments could find the money out of the travel budget. Jerry had made a small scene, and he and Evelyn had left early. Over coffee at the Salisbury House, she suggested that it was time to make their relationship more intimate. Jerry nearly panicked. He argued that his separation was too recent, that he didn't think he could enter a relationship like that for a while. He needed time to heal.

Evelyn was sympathetic. She didn't want to put pressure on him. But it was over a year now, and she thought she had to say something.

When he got back home, the girl, Debbie, was no longer sitting on the step. She was sleeping in the garage on a pile of clothes. He woke her up and told her to come inside. He put her in Margaret's room and told her that she could stay the night, but that she would have to leave in the morning.

The next morning, he could hear her splashing in the bathtub, singing a Joni Mitchell number about clouds. She was in there for a very long time, and finally, Jerry knocked on the door.

"I've got to get to work," he told her.

"Oh, I'm sorry," she answered, and she opened the door and came out into the hallway naked. She smelled of perfume and powder, and she was so beautiful that Jerry was powerfully aroused. It was an effort not to reach out and touch her. She stood there for a moment, as if she were expecting him to do just that, then she disappeared into Margaret's room.

It was not fair, Jerry decided as he ran an extra two miles at the gym. She had known precisely what she was doing. Well, he told the Nautilus machine silently, she was not going to get away with it. If she was still there when he got back he was throwing her unceremoniously out the door.

At the university, Thelma had already left her message, so he got no chance to denounce her. Mrs. Simmons next door had called. Jerry was lighting fires in the back yard. Was he a pyromaniac as well? When the time came, she'd know what to do.

Evelyn came by to see him. She apologized for last night. She hadn't realized how badly he'd been hurt in his marriage. She could wait. She'd try to help him any way she could.

His class in Canadian poetry was his smallest class. It was also composed entirely of girls. Most of them were quite beautiful, and all of them were ardent feminists. He was doing a unit on love poetry, and they were resisting. Every poem he read them they claimed was sexist, full of patriarchal desires for ownership of the loved woman. Even the love poems by women were suspect, since they merely reinforced the old stereotypes. Finally, in despair, he asked them what they wanted in a love relationship. Their answers were so vague, and when he could understand them, so stereotyped and conventional, that he decided to ask to be let off teaching the poetry course next year.

And she was still there when he came home. The house gleamed. All the little kitschy wall decorations were up again, not quite in the original order but close enough. Margaret's room now contained all the stuffed animals, and all the clothes were back in her closet. There was no sign of the girl, and Jerry breathed a sigh of relief. He was glad that she had brought back all the clothes and stuffed animals. It would save him from having to confront tears at some future meeting with daughters.

Jerry mixed himself a Scotch and soda and took the newspaper into the living room. He turned on the television set to catch the news. Unspeakable things were happening in countries with hyphenated Russian names. Another he-man movie star had died from AIDS. Deeper layers of scandal and despair had descended on the royal family. At the sight of the royal corgis sporting on the lawn, he remembered Rover. He hadn't fed the animal for days, hadn't even seen him since yesterday morning. Maybe he had run away, and someone had taken him in as a stray. Though he knew that even the greatest of canine fanatics would not take in Rover as a stray.

The dog was tied in the back yard, a fresh bowl of water beside him. He wagged his great ugly tail and whimpered in recognition. Jerry patted him on the head, and the dog responded as if that had been an actual demonstration of love. When he went back into the house, he could smell liver frying.

"What do you think you're doing?' he asked Debbie. She was dressed in a frilly dress, as if she were about to leave for a party.

"Making supper. Only all I had was that twenty dollars, so it couldn't be very fancy. Do you like liver?"

"Yes, I like liver. But you can't stay here. You've to go home."

"I don't have any home."

"What about your brothers and sisters? What about your parents?"

"I haven't got any brothers and sisters. My parents split up when I was sixteen. My mom went to Australia to live with this guy and my dad lives on a research station in the Arctic. He hardly ever comes home. I can't go and see them. I don't even have their addresses. Do you want red wine or white wine?"

"Red," Jerry told her with resignation. "But it's impossible. You can't stay here."

She finished setting the table and she came and stood very close to him. She was not large, but her presence seemed to fill the room.

"Do you want to sleep with me?" she asked. "Would that make it easier?"

"No," he roared, though that was a lie. "And you should be ashamed of even suggesting it."

"Why?" she asked. "Don't you find me attractive?"

"That's not the question," Jerry said.

"It's exactly the question," she told him. "If you throw me out, what am I going to do? I don't have any money. I don't know anybody. Sooner or later, I'll have to sleep with someone. It may as well be you and save a lot of trouble."

"I am not taking on a concubine," Jerry said. "I'm old enough to be your father. Why don't you get a job?"

"Good idea. First thing in the morning, I'll go look for one."

"I'm serious," Jerry told her. "You can stay here for a couple of days until you can find a job. But that's it."

"Agreed," she said, and they shook hands. Jerry noticed that she had the most beautiful complexion he had ever seen. The skin on her neck was as smooth as an apple.

They sat down to supper and ate in an awkward silence. After a minute or two, Debbie said, "Oh, you had some phone calls. Somebody named Thelma called. A very rude lady."

Jerry swallowed hard. "What did you tell her?"

"I told her you were out. I told her I did not know when you were expected. I told her to try again on Thursday."

"Didn't she ask who you were?"

"I said I was the maid. I told her I was cleaning up the place, and that was true. I was cleaning."

"And who else?"

"A guy threatened to murder the dog if he dug up his flower bed one more time. So I tied him in the back. By the way, what's his name?"

"Mr. Simmons. Alf Simmons."

"Your dog is named Alf Simmons?"

"No. The neighbour. The dog is named Rover."

"Rover," she said. "That's an interesting name for a dog. Most of the people I know name their dogs things like Jean Paul or Morrison. Rover's a good name for a dog."

"Yes, it is," Jerry said, mustering all the irony he could. "It's original, but appropriate, we thought."

"Like in the song," Debbie said. "The Irish Rover. That must be why he digs up other people's flower beds."

Dessert was canned pears. Jerry had never actually eaten pears out of a can before, and he was surprised to find they were not unpleasant.

"Oh. And Margaret phoned. Collect from New Brunswick, but I accepted the charges. Turned out she did remember me. We met in Calgary."

"What did she have to say?"

"Nothing. We chatted about old times."

THE NEXT MORNING, JERRY PUNISHED the Nautilus machine until it begged for mercy. He had got up in the middle of the night to go to the bathroom and found Debbie naked there, painting her toenails red. Then in the morning, she joined him for breakfast in shortie pajamas that inflamed him further. He had warned her that she was not safe dressed like that, but all she answered was that if he wanted to, he mmm, like could, you know? He wondered why he didn't take her up on her offer. He certainly wanted to. But the world, he thought, needs some sort of moral order. And if he began by seducing young women in economic need, who could imagine the future?

It turned out that Margaret did have something to say, after all. When Jerry got to the office, the phone was ringing. He waited until the machine answered and prepared himself for Thelma. Instead Margaret began, "Listen, Dad, answer the phone or I'm jumping on an airplane and coming home right now, and you are going to pay for it."

He answered the phone.

"What is Debbie doing living in your house?" she asked.

"It's your fault," he told her. "She came to visit you. Now she's got no money, and she won't go away."

"Get rid of her, Dad. I'm serious. This woman is dynamite. She's famous. There's a picture of her in *Time* magazine walking naked through a rock concert. Wherever she goes, there's disaster."

15

"She's your friend, not mine," Jerry said. "And I'd noticed that habit of walking around undressed."

"She's not my friend. She's only someone I met once at a campground. And she's not a young girl. She's about twenty-six years old. Look, Dad, if you get involved with her, I'm going to kill myself."

"Don't worry," Jerry told her. "She'll make you a good mother." And he hung up the phone slowly, cutting off what sounded like screams at the other end.

The red light on the phone was still flashing, so he listened to the other messages. Rhonda, the English Department secretary, reminding him to get in his assessment of Orest Ryhorchuk's MA proposal. Orest was a sincere but unimaginative young man who had left Phys. Ed. for English. A blockhead, Jerry thought. In a more honest period in history, he would have been regarded as a blockhead. He wanted to write a feminist psychoanalytic study of the erotica of Anaïs Nin, a project doomed from the start when undertaken by a farm boy designed to play football. Then three names he didn't know, followed by phone numbers and a reminder of the promotion meeting for the Religion Department.

Jerry groaned. The Religion Department only had three members, each of whom took a turn at being department head. They were all assistant professors, because each time one of them applied for promotion, the other two turned him down. Meetings of the promotion committee for Religion were the most bitter and acrimonious on the campus.

Jerry decided not to go. He was phoning the Dean's secretary to leave his regrets, an unavoidable trip to the dentist, he had decided, when he caught sight of Thelma and her cohort making their way across the parking lot. Thelma was as usual in flowing robes, her friend Elena dressed as a Scottish earl in hunting garb. All tweed, including the hat, and a large carved walking stick. Jerry dropped the phone and headed down the back stairs for the meeting.

The Dean thanked Jerry for making the meeting but informed him that it was postponed. They couldn't get a quorum. Only the two members of the Religion Department and Jerry had been able to make it. Everybody else had suddenly come down with dental problems. The two Religion professors glared at each other across the table. Kleinholtz, who had written a book on Karl Barth, was a large man with a terrible complexion who reminded Jerry of the Pardoner in *Canterbury Tales*. Rosenby, who wrote articles about Post-Christian America, had for no apparent reason taken to carrying an emergency medical kit, and he was carrying it now. The only thing on which the two men agreed was that come hell or high water, their colleague, Pyncheon, was not going to be promoted. Pyncheon's chief fault, it appeared, was a naïve Christian faith, which was out of place in a Religion Department.

On his way back to his office, Jerry stopped off at the bookstore, and Thelma caught him there in the new paperback fiction section where the shelves were too high to see over. She and Elena had used a pincer movement, blocking both ends of the aisle so he could not escape.

"Margaret phoned," she began. "She says you're living in sin with a woman less than half your age?"

"More than half my age. I'm only fifty. She's at least twenty-six."

"And I suppose you brutalize her too?"

"Whips and chains," Jerry said. "But she likes it. I let her buy her own whips."

"May I remind you that I still own half of that house? I want that woman out, and I want her out right away. You're enough of an embarrassment to the girls without making more of a fool of yourself." Elena nodded grimly in her tweeds at the far end of the aisle. No escape there.

"I've got an idea," Jerry said. "Why don't you go and talk to her? Maybe you could convince her that it would be in her own best interest to move out."

"You don't fool me for a second," Thelma said. "I may just do that, and you might be surprised at the results. You don't know much about women."

Jerry whispered a silent amen to that. He pleaded an upcoming class, and, to his surprise, Thelma let him go without making a scene. As soon as he was free, he circled back outside past the window until he was face to face with Elena. He stuck out his tongue at her and waggled his fingers in his ears. She looked back at him with undisguised contempt.

Elena was a poet. The worst poet in Canada, Jerry had argued back in the days when he still lived with Thelma and Elena was only a tenor in the choir. She wrote explicit lesbian love poems, most of them with the word tongue in the title. In fact, her best-known collection was called *Tongue-Titled*. It argued that lesbians constituted a new, authentic aristocracy. Thelma had wanted Jerry to put Elena's books on his poetry course, but he had refused then, and he still refused. Anyone who used the phrase "phallogocentric lust" in a poem was beyond the pale.

Back at the college, Evelyn was waiting for him. As soon as he closed his door, she knocked on it and he let her in. He saw in a second that something was wrong. As little as he knew about women, he did know enough to sense when they were angry. Still, he greeted her cheerfully, hoping he might bluff his way out of whatever crisis had occurred.

"I called your place this morning," she said. "I hoped we might meet for breakfast."

"I was gone early," he said. "Exercise." And he patted his stomach.

"A woman answered the phone."

"Debbie," he said. "A friend of my daughter Margaret. Just staying for a few days until she finds a place of her own here."

"She was asleep," Evelyn said, a note of almost hysterical accusation in her voice. "The only bed with a phone beside it is yours." Jerry wasn't sure how Evelyn knew this fact. She had visited at his house, but he had never shown her his bedroom. He decided to make nothing of this fact.

"She was up when I left," he said. "Eating toast in the kitchen. She always sounds like she just woke up. She says *ummm* a lot, and she doesn't finish her sentences."

"She seemed very confused."

"Kids," Jerry said, in a voice that was intended to indicate that the matter was settled. Evelyn was not quite prepared to let it go so quickly.

"I asked her who she was. I thought she might be one of your daughters come home unexpectedly. She said she was a friend of yours."

"Well, I guess she is. She's a friend of my daughter, so she's a friend of mine. Anyway, she can't leave fast enough for me. I've finally reclaimed the bathroom from two generations of women, and I'm not giving it up very easily again."

Evelyn smiled. She seemed relieved, though she must have noticed that the claim on the bathroom also excluded her.

"Anyway, I wanted to talk to you about Orest's thesis. Dave asked me to be external advisor on it. It sounds really exciting." Dave was Dave Anderson, who taught the critical theory course. He lived in a rarefied atmosphere of French philosophical notions and sent out bewildering memos that no one in the entire department could understand.

"Orest is a blockhead," Jerry said. "And so is Anderson if he thinks that Orest can do a feminist psychoanalysis of a book of bad pornography."

"It's not bad pornography. And why can't Orest do it?"

"Okay. If you say it's good pornography, it's good pornography. But Orest doesn't know the faintest thing about the way a woman's mind works. He's a good inside tackle, and he should have kept to that. Or written about Irony in Robertson Davies. If he tries this the feminists will eat him alive."

"I didn't say it was good pornography. It's not pornography at all. And Orest doesn't have to know how a woman's mind works. He just has to deal with the evidence in the text. I don't see any reason why he couldn't do the topic."

"Good," Jerry said. "It's done then. Orest analyzes why women think dirty thoughts." He pulled the form out of the pile of forms on his desk, signed it and slipped it into an envelope.

"You missed the college meeting this morning," Evelyn went on. "We've decided to go ahead with the weekend retreat out to Maple Lake to talk over the future of the college."

"What?" Jerry asked. "A dirty weekend with these guys?" and he swept his hand to take in the entire building. Maple Lake advertised itself as a place to get away to and renew your relationship. It didn't say "marriage," so as not to discriminate against other sorts of union. "I thought that idea had been wastebasketted weeks ago."

"Not so. The Rector found some money. We leave a week from Friday."

"Why doesn't he put it into the photocopying budget? Or upgrade the quality of the toilet paper? Something that would make a real difference to our lives."

"*C'est la vie*," Evelyn told him, walking out the door. "Got to go and pack for the big holiday."

Jerry stirred the mess of papers and unopened letters on his desk. Colby's letter came to the top again. Colby was his old college roommate who had gone off to Australia and made a fortune. Once a year he wrote Jerry a letter bragging about his wealth and offering Jerry a job in Australia. He remembered Colby as a huge man with an enormous sexual appetite who always got what he wanted. For some reason that Jerry did not quite comprehend, Colby maintained a deep and consistent affection for him, even though Jerry never answered his letters. This letter had "urgent" written on the envelope in red ink. Jerry put it into the large drawer on his desk, the drawer from which nothing ever returned. Jerry felt sufficiently inadequate on his own without having to measure up to Colby.

On impulse, Jerry decided to phone home. Since Margaret's phone call he had been brooding on her description of Debbie as a walking disaster. Still, what could she have done? Sunbathed naked in the back yard and scandalized all the neighbours, probably.

The phone rang several times before Debbie picked it up. Jerry knew the machine would answer after four rings, so he hung up after three and dialled again. The fourth time he dialled, he got through.

"Yuh," Debbie said. "King residence, maid speaking."

"Were you sunbathing naked in the back yard?" Jerry asked her.

"Yuh," she said. "How did you know?"

"Just a lucky guess. Everything all right there?"

"Fine. A couple of people tried to break in, but I called the police and they took them away."

"What kind of people?"

"I don't know. People. A man and a woman. Funny guy in a tweed suit with a walking stick. They were peeking at me through the fence, and when I went inside, they sneaked into the basement, so I called the police."

"Do you remember anything they said?"

"Yeah. The lady said she owned the house, but I told the police it was yours."

"Thanks," Jerry said. "That's terrific."

"Did I do something wrong?"

"No," Jerry said. "Everything is hunky dory."

He hung up the phone and put his feet on the desk and waited for it to ring. In about thirty seconds it did that.

"Welcome to my office, Thelma, you old bitch," he told the ringing telephone as he waited for the beep and her voice. But it wasn't Thelma. It was Anderson calling to see if he wanted to go for a beer on the way home. He picked up the phone and apologized.

"Sorry, Dave. I just got in and the machine had already answered."

"You don't fool anyone," Anderson told him. "The only way to get you to answer is to promise you beer. But in this case I wasn't trying to flush you out. I actually would like to see you."

"Promise we won't talk about Orest and the ladies?"

"Promise."

"And Heidegger is out of the question? No deconstruction, hermeneutics or semiotics?

"I won't draw a serious breath. We can talk about the Saskatchewan Roughriders."

"Okay, as long as it isn't technical. Where?"

Anderson suggested Gert's, a place near the university that attracted mostly the greying faculty but insisted on thinking of itself as a sports bar. There was rarely a person in it capable of doing ten push-ups. Jerry started to pack his briefcase. He'd given a brief test a couple of weeks ago, and he still hadn't marked the papers. The students were starting to get a little restless. Still, by the time he'd had a couple of beers and sorted out the mess at home, he wasn't going to be in any mood for marking. He emptied the papers back out onto his desk.

The phone rang and he jumped. This time it was Thelma. "Answer the goddamn phone," she said. "Don't hide in there like a cringing coward." She paused. When it was clear that Jerry was not going to answer, she went on. "That woman has got to go. She called the police on us today. I want you to remember that I still own half of that house." Jerry moved to the door and opened it as she went on. She gave him the name of her lawyer and had begun explaining what action she and the girls were going to take when Jerry whispered, "'Bye, Love," and pulled the door closed behind him. He could hear her talking all the way to the end of the hall, though he could not make out what she was saying.

"You know how men get to be professors?" Jerry said to Anderson. They had ordered a large pitcher of beer, and it had come with big mugs, fresh from the freezer and covered with ice. "They get to be professors through the Law of Natural Incompetence. As children, they're so socially maladapted that no one will play with them. They're so physically inept that they never make the teams. The only thing left to them, the only way they can succeed, is by studying and brown-nosing the teacher. Then later in high school they're so ugly that they can't get any dates, and so they have to stay home and study. The bright athletic guys knock up their beautiful girlfriends in grade twelve and go on to make fortunes as bakers and plumbers. The nerds go on studying and brown-nosing until finally they get their PhDs. They wake up one day, and they're thirty years old, they're still virgins, they don't know how to dress themselves and they're teaching a graduate course in Particle

Physics. And in front of them are the next generation of nerds. And these guys disgust them as much as they disgust themselves, so they brutalize the little creeps. It's a bizarre natural phenomenon."

"But they're married," Anderson reminded him. "All those guys get married."

"Have you noticed how incredibly ugly their wives are? That's because these are the left-over women, the ones that couldn't get the bakers and the plumbers. They've about given up hope, and they lower their standards and pick off a ripe nerd. I don't want to be sexist about this though. There are also socially and physically inept female professors with ugly husbands. It works both ways."

"You've been talking to Thelma again," Anderson said. "Talking with Thelma always brings you to a certain hysterical eloquence."

"They're mad," Jerry said. "I don't know if you've noticed, but all the women in the world have gone mad in the last few years."

"It's called liberation," Anderson told him. "There's a movement called feminism that you might have read about. Something about trying to change two million years of oppression."

"Don't tell me about feminism," Jerry said. "I am an expert on feminism. A survivor from the early wars. Badly wounded, missing in action for a while, but still surviving. My wife ran off with a woman with more hair on her chest than I have on mine. I have three daughters, just like King Lear, only they're all ungrateful. Evelyn is trying to get me into her bed, but if I wake up in the night with an erection, I can get rid of it by thinking about Evelyn. And now I have a re-tread hippie living in my house, walking around naked and enraging the neighbours."

Anderson was interested in this new development and

Jerry told him about it in some detail, including Debbie's offer.

"Screw her," Anderson said. "She's free and liberated. She makes her own choices. If she wants you to screw her and has specifically made the request, then the act does not constitute sexual harassment. It says so in the university handbook."

"I can't," Jerry said. "She's walking around in my daughter's nightgown. It would seem like incest."

"You're fifty," Anderson said. "You're afraid you wouldn't be able to get it up. It's called a mid-life crisis."

"Thanks," Jerry told him. "Hey, how about them Roughriders. Fifty-five to fourteen the other night."

"Yeah, but they got the fourteen."

"Still, it's an improvement. They're starting to score."

By the time they left, they had drunk two full pitchers, and Jerry wasn't sure he should be driving. Getting breathalyzed and losing his licence would be more than he could bear. And Anderson did have a motive. The graduate studies committee needed a new chair, and they wanted Jerry to be it.

Jerry protested. He said he hated graduate students because they reminded him of his own wasted youth. He protested that he couldn't keep files and he always missed appointments.

"And besides," he said to Anderson, "why are you asking me? Why hasn't the Commander himself offered me this lovely plum?"

The Commander was James Harper, head of the department and busy yachtsman. He was reputed to have once been a professional wrestler, and given his size, it was not unlikely. But no one had ever found stronger evidence than his Darth Vader belt buckle. He rarely made personal appearances and conducted all his business by memo or through Anderson, who to all appearances seemed to run the department. Jerry had recently accused Anderson of killing the Commander and hiding his body in the faculty lounge where it could go unnoticed for years.

"The Commander does not like you, Jerry," Anderson said. "The Commander likes order and obedience. He sees you as the embodiment of chaos and disrespect. If he could find anybody else he would not give you this position of authority and power."

"So you think I should take it to spite him?"

"It's the way we usually do business."

By the time they'd finished their beer, Jerry had tentatively agreed to think about it, saying he would decide next week.

When he got home, Debbie was not there. Jerry felt oddly disappointed. He considered Anderson's advice. Anderson was almost certainly correct. If it was part of the bargain that she sleep with him, then so be it.

The parakeet was loose, and it had shat on the couch again. Jerry found an old hat, chased the parakeet into a corner, and caught it in his hat. He hated to touch birds. They were fragile and vicious at the same time. He put the parakeet back in its cage, and tried to clean off the couch with a wet rag. The couch looked even worse by the time he had thoroughly rubbed the birdshit into it.

The dog was not in the yard. He looked everywhere for it, walking down the lane calling its hateful name without success. Finally, Jerry found it lying on his bed in a nest of its own fur. He cursed it and it limped out into the yard where it howled in remorse until he relented and allowed it into the basement.

Then the phone rang. He picked it up without waiting for the machine, hoping it might be Thelma. He was angry enough now to yell at her in person. But it wasn't Thelma. It was Cindy, calling from Pincher Creek.

"I thought you said you didn't want to talk to me," Jerry

said. "I thought this particular relationship was dead in the water."

"I said don't you call. I didn't say I wouldn't call."

"Sorry. How's the cowboy?"

"Pete?"

"Have you got more than one?"

"Don't be sarcastic. That's one of your problems. You can never treat things seriously. Irony is your specialty."

"Actually, I specialize in litotes. Irony is only a sideline."

"See what I mean? Anyway," and here her voice dropped in pitch to indicate that there would be no more joking, "Pete's pretty busy with the round-up. And I've been riding with him. There's a lot of work to a ranch. So I just heard from Mom about your latest escapade."

"And which one is that?"

"You know what I'm talking about. The bimbo you've got living with you. Mom was not very happy about that little incident with the police."

"She'll have to break that habit of breaking into houses then," Jerry told her. "She's running with a pretty mean crowd, and there's not much I can do about it."

"And I don't want her wearing my clothes. Mom said she was wearing my dress and Lise's sweater."

"You don't fit your clothes anymore. You've got too bulky from all that fresh air and sirloin steak. Besides, I was giving them to the Salvation Army, and she rescued them from the box. Finder's keepers."

"Dad, I want those clothes. They fit me fine. Get them back from her. Pete and me are going to drive out in a couple of weeks, and I'm going to take them back with me."

The back door opened, and Debbie called out, "Jerry? Are you there?"

"Is that her?" Cindy asked. "Is that your bimbo? Put her on the phone and let me talk to her."

"That's just the television," Jerry said. "Look, I got to run. I've got a bunch of papers to mark. Say hi to the cowperson for me. And don't fall off any horses." He hung up before she could reply.

"I got an interview," Debbie said. "In fact I got two interviews." She was dressed exactly as Cindy had described her, in Cindy's black dress and Lise's yellow sweater.

"Great," Jerry said. "When?"

"Next week. Thursday. Then the Tuesday after that."

Jerry calculated. She could be with him for nearly two weeks, but should be gone before Cindy arrived.

"What kind of jobs?"

"Well, the first one is as financial officer at the credit union. And the other is as bursar at the college. I put you down as a reference. Is that okay?"

Jerry's heart sank. He didn't know what he had expected. Waitress, probably. Or cash-out clerk at the supermarket. There was no chance she could get these jobs, and so no chance of her leaving.

"I can't give you a reference," Jerry said. "I don't know anything about you. Do you have any qualifications?"

"I've got an MBA from Western," she said. "I can do these jobs. They're horrible, hateful, shitty jobs, but I can do them. Okay?"

"When did you find time to do an MBA? I thought you were a hippie."

Debbie laughed. "You guys were the hippies. My parents were hippies for a while. I'm just an ordinary southern Ontario girl with a few miles on the road. You know. Travelling?"

Jerry did not know. It made no sense at all. Suddenly the whole situation had shifted. Debbie had all the power now. And he could not sleep with an MBA. That, at least, was out of the question.

THE NEXT MORNING, JERRY CAME DOWN to breakfast tired and confused. He had been unable to sleep, tossing fitfully and dreaming complex dreams about finance, RRSPs, and guaranteed investment certificates. It seemed he was being forced to retire, and he did not have enough money to live. Debbie was already there, curled up in a chair in Margaret's shortie pajamas, reading the financial pages of the paper.

"Got to keep in trim," she said. "Got to get the old brain clicking numbers so I can make an honest living."

Jerry was no match for the Nautilus machine. It beat him hands down, and left him a sweaty wreck. He got a stitch in his side running, and quit before he'd completed a mile. When he got to the university a line-up of students was waiting at his door. Apparently the department secretary, buoyed up by Anderson's report that he had not actually refused the job, had decided to send all the graduate students to him.

The first one was Norma Jean Shepard, a tiny, pretty girl with a deep, husky voice. She wanted to switch from an MA in Renaissance to a creative writing thesis. Jerry phoned her supervisor, Bill Chamberlain, who, though balding and intense, was nevertheless the youngest member of the department.

"She can't do this to me," Chamberlain practically screamed into the phone. "She's already finished the thesis. I've worked with her for two years on this. All she has to do is revise the conclusion, and it's done. Now she wants to write a stupid novel. Look, tell her she doesn't even have to revise the conclusion. It's good enough as it stands. I'll set up an oral exam for next week, and she can have her MA."

Norma refused. She'd lost all interest in the Renaissance. All she wanted to do was write a novel about a football team. She knew nothing about football, but she was prepared to do the work. In a moment of inspiration, Jerry worked out a compromise. He asked each side for a month's waiting period before a firm decision was made. Then he talked to the department secretary and assigned Norma to share an office with Orest. She could do her research without leaving the room, and Orest might find out something about female sexual fantasies.

The second student was a Chinese from Manchuria. His student visa had run out, and he wanted Jerry to sign a form saying his progress was satisfactory. He had been around for two years, and, as it turned out, had never handed in a single paper. He had voluntarily withdrawn from every course at the last minute. When Jerry refused to sign the form, he said that he could not go back because he would be imprisoned for his stand on the Tiananmen Square issue. He vowed to commit suicide in front of Jerry's office rather than return. Jerry sent him to the student appeals committee.

The other requests were all quite simple. Everybody wanted to do something that was expressly forbidden by the rules of the department. Jerry thought of the endless meetings and reviews he would have to sit through if he denied the requests. He granted them all and in ten minutes cleared up about six months' work.

Evelyn dropped by his office.

"Congratulations. I hear you've been made head of the graduate committee."

"There," Jerry told her, "is ample evidence of the evils of alcohol. I had a couple of beers with Anderson, and, because I failed to make an iron-clad refusal, I find myself appointed. Despite my clearly demonstrated incompetence as an administrator. I cannot organize my way out of a paper bag. Also this is not news. Everybody in the department acknowledges my inability to get anything done on time."

"Clearly, presidential material," Evelyn said. "I can see it all now. Next year, Dean of Arts. The year after, Academic

Vice-President, then, through the tragic death of the President, the big office in the rotunda. Only I wouldn't brag so much about my qualifications. It isn't seemly."

"You're right," Jerry said. "Only I hadn't thought about it that way. I'll work hard and do such a good job that they'll drop me like a hot potato. What's new?"

"You all gassed up, ready for the big trip? Have you put together all your great ideas for the future of the college?"

"Oh Christ! Not already?"

"This very afternoon. We're leaving in a convoy at four."

"There's no way. I can't possibly do it."

But he did. He got a ride with Evelyn and a plump sociologist named Beryl. Beryl was the sort of person you had to look at twice to see that she was not wearing a mask. Jerry thought she bore a remarkable resemblance to the singer Tiny Tim, only she was shorter and fat. She said she was terrified of driving cars and insisted on sitting in the back seat.

Already Jerry regretted having been bullied by the Rector into accepting this arrangement for what the Rector called "green reasons." Jerry had wanted to take his little red Mazda Miata, his one indulgence since Thelma had left, but the Rector had insisted that they all share the larger vehicles. A two-seater was out of the question.

One of the reasons Jerry had wanted to take the Mazda was that if things got too boring, he could slip away early. He suspected that the Rector's decision to bundle his staff together was to prevent just such action, rather than any great concern for the environment.

Debbie had not been home when he arrived to pack a suitcase, but he left her a note, explaining in perhaps too much detail where he was. He had even left her a map, though he wasn't sure why.

Now, they sped up Highway 8 towards Maple Leaf Lodge. Beryl turned out to be an expert on Hutterites, and since they had to pass a Hutterite colony on the way, she got a chance to open her subject. Jerry had learned never to allow a fellow academic to discuss his specialty. Or in this case her specialty. For some reason he had thought she specialized in the urban poor, and by the time he caught on it was too late. She was well launched, and she lectured them for the full two hours of the trip on the history, care and feeding of Hutterites, including a couple of jokes that must have made at least two generations of students moan.

The lodge itself was quite beautiful. It was on the shore of the lake beside a large golf course. Hiking trails, which in winter would become cross-country ski trails, led in all directions. His room turned out to be between Evelyn and Beryl's, as if all the travel arrangements had been made far in advance. The room was simple: a bed, a small dresser with mirror, a couple of chairs and a small refrigerator packed with booze. It was not a serious drinker's fridge, Jerry reflected. There was one of everything. Anyone intending on getting drunk on the contents would probably get sick before he got drunk.

After supper, Jerry slipped away from the get-acquainted party early. Everybody wore name tags, even though the only people who hadn't been in the college for ten years were the receptionist and the new young woman from Women's Studies. The receptionist was named Mary Jane something-or-other, and she appeared never to have heard of the women's movement. She was so helpful and so willing to do things beyond her job description that it embarrassed everybody. She went up to the lounge every morning and brought the Rector tea at ten o'clock. If anyone else were present when this happened, he would shrug his shoulders as if this were a fact of nature about which he could do nothing.

The New Woman, as Jerry called her to himself, was

named Willie Barker. Her masculine name, and the fact that Thelma and Elena had welcomed her appointment with glee, had made Jerry avoid her at every opportunity. Her dress was not mannish, but it was not feminine either. Though she was only about thirty years old, she contrived to look like somebody's old aunt.

In a brief introduction, the coordinator, a young man from Pittsburgh, explained the concept. These next two days were to be democratic. Everybody was to be equal, whatever their title or position was in the ordinary world. They were to address each other by their first names. He understood that the college was not exactly a business, but the patterns still worked. They had a product to sell. They took in raw materials, the students, and they moulded this material in the most efficient ways they could to produce a product that was saleable, that is to say, graduates who could get jobs. Everybody from the cleaners to the leader, and here the Rector smiled, made a contribution. Tomorrow, they would each describe what they did, express their frustrations frankly and without offense. Then on Sunday they would talk about how to put together a better team. Now, it was time to really get to know each other.

Jerry had been edging toward the door as this little speech went on, and as soon as it was over, he slipped out. He found the nearest hiking trail and ran down it in a gentle jog. When he thought he was far enough ahead that no one would catch him, he slowed to a walk. The path followed the lake, fairly large waves crashed in, making a muffled roar, and the trees formed a canopy over his head. The leaves had started to turn yellow and red, though it was still only October. After about a half hour, he found a large rock that stood out in the water, but which could be reached by a small leap. He made the leap and settled down to think.

He realized that he missed Debbie, even though he had

seen her only that morning. It was insane, of course. He would
have to get rid of her as soon as possible. Still, when she was
gone, the house would be empty again. And he had begun to
have sex fantasies again. After Thelma had left, he had given
up even fantasy. Now, this woman had said that she would
sleep with him, and the very thought stirred him. At the same
time, it was impossible. She was much too young. And he
didn't want anyone sleeping with him out of gratitude. The
problem was that the alternative was love, and he certainly
didn't want to get involved with love again. Certainly not yet.
If ever. He thought of her curled up in the shortie pajamas with
her bright red toenails, smelling of bath powder and perfume.

He heard a cough behind him and turned. It was the New
Woman.

"Mind if I join you?" she said, and made the leap to the
rock.

Jerry did mind. He minded most emphatically, but he
didn't have the nerve to say so.

"No," he said. "It's a free country." Then realizing how
mean that sounded, he added, "By all means. Make yourself
at home."

"Does this happen all the time?" she asked.

At first Jerry thought she meant his sitting on rocks by the
edge of a lake reflecting on his sex life, but he realized this
could not be. She must mean the retreat.

"No," he said. "This is the first time." His answer could
have stood for either question.

"I can't believe it," she went on. "A whole roomful of
adults is going to play charades for two days?"

"Not for two days," Jerry told her. "For weeks and years,
on *ad infinitum*, until the final candle is blown out."

"That's very poetic," she said. "Do you write poetry?"

"No," he said. "I leave that to my ex-wife and her buddy.
I was thinking of Macbeth."

"Thelma and Elena?"

"The very ones."

"What a pair of monsters," the woman went on. "They want me to teach Elena's poetry. First, I don't teach poetry if I can help it, and second, her poetry is crap. They're relentless. They phone me every day. They send me memos. They invite me to parties."

Jerry looked at the woman with a new interest. Apparently they shared more than he had suspected. "Do you go?"

"No. Of course not. I'm not into redefining my sexuality. They talk about you a lot, though. Apparently you're something of a monster."

"It's true," Jerry said ruefully. "I am a monster. No woman is safe with me around."

"And yet the police let you walk around unmolested, as it were."

"Yes. It's a flaw in the system. Mind you, I only do psychological damage. I never raise a hand in anger. But I have an ex-wife and three ex-daughters who will testify to my brutality."

"How do you accomplish this?"

"Neglect, mostly. Failure to be there when I am needed. Irony. Hypocritical self-righteousness. That sort of thing."

"Nothing more specific than that?"

"They accuse me of paternalism. But damnit I am the father. I thought that was what the job was all about."

"Don't worry," she said. "They'll grow out of it. Even Thelma, I suspect. It's a popular position at the moment. Fathers are not a growth stock. They're being sold short at the moment."

The woman had her hair pinned back so that it pulled the skin tight on her face. Her glasses were quite thick, so that from an angle he could see the rings in the glass. "Why do they call you Willie?" he asked.

"It's short for Wilhelmina. My father wanted a boy, but all he got was six daughters. In the end he called me Willie and gave up trying."

"Did you try to be like a boy to make him happy?"

"Yes. I climbed trees, and played hockey and collected stamps. I always took dares and I fixed things. Then one day he died, and there was no more reason for doing any of that."

Willie turned away from Jerry and began to pull the pins from her hair. It tumbled down softly over her shoulders. She took off her glasses and put them on the rock as she combed her hair into shape with her fingers. Then she turned to Jerry, her eyes wide and near-sighted, and a little too close to him. Jerry could not resist. She was startlingly beautiful in the fading light. He leaned over and kissed her.

She seemed both to accept the kiss and to jump back startled.

"Why did you do that?"

"I don't know. You looked so beautiful. I didn't intend to. It just happened," he finished lamely.

"Well, I think we'd better leave it at that," she said. "I think it's time to be getting back."

They walked back in silence. Jerry didn't know whether he had been reprimanded or simply postponed. They parted in the lobby of the lodge.

"Good night, Doctor King," she said.

"Good night, Doctor Barker," he answered.

THE NEXT MORNING, Willie appeared at breakfast in a soft dark gown, her long hair flowing down over her shoulders. Jerry thought she looked edible. Her complexion was impossibly smooth, and her glasses seemed not protective as they had before, but simply some exotic form of decoration.

She sat a couple of tables away with the Rector and a philosopher named Watkins who could have acted the part of Ichabod Crane in any theatrical production. The men struck Jerry as leering and offensive, especially the Rector, who had dribbled a little milk down his chin and not noticed it.

Jerry was sitting with Evelyn and Beryl. Beryl had tried to introduce Hutterites into the conversation, but Jerry had relentlessly hauled the topic away from her. Now, in the moment of his distraction, she seized the floor again and began to describe the practice of communal cooking and shared responsibility.

Evelyn had not failed to see the source of Jerry's distraction, and when Beryl paused to eat another spoonful of her grapefruit, she struck.

"It's a pity," she said. "Such a waste."

"What do you mean?"

"Oh, just that it must seem a pity to you men that such a beautiful woman as Willie should have chosen her own sex over yours."

"What do you mean? She's gay?"

"It's not particularly a secret. She wrote an article on lesbian women in the academic world."

"What does that mean?" Jerry said. "I could write an article on the topic, and I'm not a lesbian."

"You better read the article."

Jerry felt his heart sink. Probably, almost certainly, Evelyn was right. It was exactly what he himself had believed until last night. Perhaps there was this flaw in him that he was drawn only to lesbians, or that any woman he touched recoiled and turned to other women. Yet he had been certain last night that the attraction had been mutual. But then he had been certain about Thelma, too.

When the sessions began, Willie had mercifully pulled back her hair and looked as distant and cold as ever. The young man from Pittsburgh had the good sense not to push the product metaphor too far. And after a few hesitant moments, the entire group loosed a barrage of complaints. Jerry was astounded that there was so much frustration and hostility hidden behind the normally good-humoured facade of the college. Professors complained that the mail was never sorted on time, and that they had to come down from their offices at awkward moments to pick it up. The receptionist who had to sort the mail complained that she had to answer the telephone and deal with anyone who came to the door, and she could not let the phone ring while she sorted. The Rector was a PC man and the Macintosh users complained that they could not use the laser printer because the network had been damaged to make it work for PCs. The professors never cleaned their feet at the door and dragged mud needlessly into their offices. There was no wheelchair access. The office was locked for an hour at noon. The air conditioning, promised twenty years ago, had still not arrived.

By noon, to Jerry's amazement, the air seemed to have cleared. Several new procedures had been developed, and everyone had promised to be more open to avoid misunderstandings. Even Macpherson from History, a relentless Scotsman with a ferocious temper and a bright red beard, had become conciliatory. At lunch, by dint of some lightning-swift manoeuvres, Jerry managed to free himself from Evelyn and Beryl and sit at the same table with Willie.

As they sat down, he whispered to her, "It's amazing, isn't it?"

"Not really. Anyone who has gone to a convent school could have predicted it. Wait till this afternoon."

That was all the conversation he got. The Rector dominated the rest of the lunch with a disquisition on fundraising and some comic stories of his efforts to raise funds in the small parish he had operated thirty years ago.

And Willie was right. After lunch, there were territories to be defended, reasons why so much of the budget had to go to one or another area. The chaplain's salary was pitifully small, though of course he did not complain. It could be made reasonable by cutting back on cultural programming and visiting speakers. On the other hand, perhaps the college could get by without a chaplain, and the cultural and visiting speakers committee could make the college a model for the whole university. By dinner it was clear that nothing was actually going to change.

AGAIN, JERRY CONTRIVED TO HAVE DINNER with Willie, and to avoid the now watchful eye of Evelyn. Jerry felt doubly unfaithful, first to Debbie, who awaited him at home, and then to Evelyn, who watched from the next table. Whoever had made the menu and designed the service had some experience with the fine restaurants of Paris. They had not, however, been able to find a chef prepared to work the backwoods, and the fish arrived burned in a sauce that bore no resemblance to the one described on the menu.

Jerry suggested a walk to Willie and she agreed. He tried to manoeuvre her to the same spot as the other night, hoping for magic, but she resisted. Instead, they walked along the edge of the golf course, avoiding the erratic shots of a few late golfers determined to squeeze out the last hours of light. On the thirteenth tee, they encountered a morose Evelyn, who swung by them wordlessly, looking like the Lady of Shallot. Willie was remarkably open. She spoke about her childhood, about her classes at the University of Toronto, about her classes at the university. She did not talk about her sexual preferences, but she did make it clear that, at least for the moment, Jerry was not one of them. It turned out that she had not been bullied by the Rector and had brought her own car, an admittedly less decadent Honda Civic, but a blight on nature nevertheless. Jerry made arrangements to get a ride back to the city with her after breakfast. The rest would stay until lunch.

Back in his room, Jerry fell immediately into a deep, dreamless sleep, which, moments later, was interrupted by a pounding at his door. He opened it, full of alarm, to discover Evelyn in her dressing gown with a bottle of Scotch in her hand. More than half of the bottle was gone.

"Let's have a drink," she said, passing him the bottle. Jerry was embarrassed, standing there in his shorts, but he soon gained his composure, slipped into a robe, found a couple of glasses and poured them each a drink. Evelyn sat on the bed and downed her drink in a single flourish. Jerry poured her another.

"Did you have a good walk?" she asked.

"It was okay. Willie's new here. She really doesn't know anybody. I was only being friendly."

"Friendly?" Evelyn snorted, as if Jerry had been caught in public fornication.

"Sure," Jerry said, and he took a long pull at his own Scotch. "Besides, like you said, you know, she's interested in her own sex, not mine."

"Maybe," Evelyn said. "Maybe. And maybe she swings both ways. Does she swing both ways, Jerry?" She got up and stood over Jerry as if she were about to hit him.

"Don't be stupid," Jerry said sharply, and she fell back onto the bed.

"It isn't fair," she said. "For a year, you ask me to be patient, then you dump me like an old rag." She began to weep noisily.

More to quiet her than anything else, Jerry sat down beside her and stroked her arms.

"I'm not dumping you. I was just talking with Willie. There is nothing more than that. I promise." He regretted the word promise the moment it left his lips. Evelyn looked up at him tearfully with eyes that wanted to believe. Then she hauled him down onto her and kissed him passionately. Jerry felt himself trapped, but there was nothing he could do. He stroked her body and lay beside her in the whiskey-scented dark. He prayed his body would not respond, but even that failed him. He could feel his erection grow. Finally, he hovered over her, looking down into her eyes, and realized that she had passed out. He rolled over onto his back, and in less than a minute he was sound asleep.

JERRY WAS UP EARLY THE NEXT MORNING. Evelyn, beside him in the bed, groaned but refused to surface into consciousness. He dressed, packed his bag and scribbled her a note saying he was sorry about last night, and he'd see her back in town. Willie was waiting for him when he got down to the lobby. They drove back to the city in early morning silence. Jerry was surprised that she tuned her radio to a country and western station, and even more surprised that she knew most of the songs and hummed along with them. He refused to raise the topic, however. He himself couldn't bear western music, but every time he got into a discussion of the topic, he came off as somehow morally inferior.

Willie did mention a man she had lived with for a couple of years, and Jerry took this as a good sign. Not proof of anything, as Thelma demonstrated, but a sign nevertheless. His name had been Doug, and he had been a vegetarian. She referred to him as "the herbivore," and said that in the end she had left him for a hunk of red meat. She had bought herself a T-bone steak and left it in the fridge. He had thrown it in the garbage. She had gone right out and bought another and cooked it immediately. He complained that it stank out the whole place, and that he would have to go somewhere else to sleep that night. He left, and while he was gone, she packed her bags and moved out before he got back. She had never even seen him again.

Willie dropped Jerry off at home. Debbie was sunbathing in the driveway in the weak October sun. She was draped in a small towel, but at least she was not stark naked. Willie looked at her with interest, but she didn't say anything.

"Friend of my daughter," Jerry told her.

"Oh," she answered in a perfectly neutral tone. Then she backed down the driveway and was gone.

"If you keep tanning, you're going to be covered with wrinkles by the time you're forty," he told Debbie.

"I'll be covered with wrinkles by the time I'm forty anyway," she answered. "After you're forty, nobody cares how you look. And in the meantime, I look better tanned."

"There's cancer. You could get cancer."

"I'll probably die of something else long before that. Evelyn phoned a few minutes ago. From Maple Lake. She was all breathy and mysterious. And Lise phones every hour on the hour. She left a number for you to call."

Jerry called. Lise was concerned. They'd had a conference call, Thelma and all the sisters. Was it true that he was living with a child?

No, Jerry told her, it was not true. Debbie was only staying for a few days until she got a job. But beyond that, it wasn't anybody's business. To his surprise, Lise agreed.

"It's your life. You've got to live it," she said. "But after you screwed up your relationship with Mom, I don't want to see you making more mistakes."

"They're my mistakes," he reminded her. "I'll make them if I want to."

Lise ignored this. "Has Mom told you about the reunion?"

"What reunion?"

"We're all going to come back home for a weekend. Sometime soon. As soon as we can work out the details."

"What do you mean, home? Do you mean here, in my house?"

"It's a lot cheaper than hotels, Dad. Try to be reasonable just this once. Anyway, we'll be in touch. I've got to run. Leon has a flight out to San Francisco in a couple of hours. I've got to drive him to the airport."

The phone was still rocking in its cradle when it rang again. Evelyn.

"Your note was sweet," she said. "But there was no need for you to apologize. It was all quite wonderful. It's me who should apologize for being such a drunk."

"You fell asleep, and . . . ," he hesitated.

"I know. I guess I sort of missed the ending. But there's no reason for you to feel guilty. There's always another time. Anyway, we can talk about it later. The Rector is furious. Everybody, including me, missed the morning session. See you at the college."

"Wait," Jerry called, but it was too late. She had hung up. He wasn't quite sure what she had said. She appeared to think he had made love to her while she slept. He would have to make it clear to her what had happened. Or rather, what had not happened. Though even that might not be very easy.

Evelyn's confusion reminded him of his mother. It was Sunday afternoon, and he hadn't visited her for a month. Since his father's death a couple of years ago, she had lived alone in the rambling old house on the river. She seemed to operate quite competently, though Jerry could never figure out how. He had tried to convince her to go into a nursing home, but she always refused. She wouldn't telephone him because she refused to talk to the answering machine. She'd had her appendix removed, and he hadn't even found out until she was home from the hospital.

He left Debbie, still covered with the towel, but now toasting another part of her anatomy, and got into the Mazda. He drove across town to the old house on the river. It had apparently been painted in the last month, a splashy, bright blue that must have offended the neighbours. He hoped she hadn't been rooked by some fly-by-night outfit.

"You're fat" was the first thing she said when she saw Jerry. "Pull yourself together, man. Get a little exercise. Are you eating right? Are you eating your vegetables?"

"I'm doing fine, Mom," he told her. "I'm eating well. I exercise every day. I haven't gained a pound in five years. In fact, I've lost weight."

"Not because of the work you do helping your mother. I've had to paint this whole place myself."

"You did not paint this place," Jerry told her. "You did not climb a thirty-foot ladder and paint the top storey of this old monstrosity."

"Oh, and who do you suppose did?"

"You hired somebody. You hired a company."

"Maybe I did. I can't remember things so good anymore. Where's your sister? Why didn't you bring your sister?"

"She's in Montreal. Carol lives in Montreal now. She's lived there for twelve years."

His mother looked at him slyly. "And how many children does she have?"

"Two," Jerry said. "Two boys. Craig and Lester."

"Three," his mother said in triumph. "They've got three. They adopted a little girl."

She was right. Jerry had forgotten. It had only been last year, and he had never seen the child.

"Right," Jerry said. "You're right."

"See that she eats her vegetables," his mother went on. "She was always too skinny. Never wanted to eat her vegetables."

"I'll see to it," Jerry said. He toured the house. Everything seemed in order. The refrigerator was well stocked, there were cans of food in the pantry, the house was clean and even the lawn was newly cut. Jerry was pleased. Maybe the nursing home could be held off for a few months.

"It's Hubert," his mother said, as if Jerry had actually asked her about the lawn. "He cuts the grass and plants flowers and he painted the house. He wants me to marry him."

Hubert was an elderly neighbour. He and his wife had played bridge with Jerry's parents for as long as he could remember, until Hubert's wife had died about ten years ago. After that, they rarely saw each other.

"He wants to marry you?" Jerry asked, playing for time.

"Yes, but he's a sex maniac. I turned him down flat."

Jerry did not want to pursue the topic of Hubert's sex manias any further, and so he tried to change the subject, but his mother would have none of it. "The man's a danger. He ought to be locked up."

"What did he do, Mother?"

"I let him use the bathroom, and he didn't even close the door. He just stood there with his thing in his hand and peed right into the middle of the bowl, making a horrible racket. Your dad always peed on the side, so it didn't make noise. He was a gentleman."

"Why were you looking at him in the bathroom, Mom?"

"People steal things. You can't be too careful. Things are always disappearing around here. How's Thelma?"

"I don't live with Thelma anymore, Mom. We're divorced."

"Good. I never liked her anyway. Great cow of a thing. You can do better than that."

Jerry persevered for nearly two hours. His mother's

lightning shifts of conversation kept him permanently off guard. When he finally got up to go, she told him, "Come again some time when you can't stay so long."

Jerry didn't take the bait, but he reflected as he drove home that any man with a mother like his should have known enough to avoid women like the plague.

THE PARAKEET WAS DEAD when Jerry got home. It had got out of its cage, and, as Jerry had always suspected would happen, it had shat so much that finally there wasn't enough of it left to sustain life. Now it lay on a blue saucer on the coffee table while Debbie wept disconsolately.

"It's only a bird," Jerry told her. "And a vile and hateful bird at that. It's going to cost two hundred dollars in dry cleaning, and I don't know if the rug can be saved."

"It's my fault," she wept. "I took him out to let him perch on my finger. Then when I put him back, I forgot to latch the door. Now his little life is gone, and it's my fault."

"He had no future anyway. I was going to wring his neck this week. I just hadn't got around to it yet."

"But you didn't. It was me who killed him." And she wept even harder.

Jerry watched her weep for a couple of minutes, then told her, "Look, if the viewing of the remains is over, I'll deposit the corpse in the garbage. I've got to do some marking and get some sleep."

"No, you don't," Debbie said, and she seized the saucer with its tiny puff of feathers. "I'll bury him in the back yard." She disappeared out the door with the bird.

Jerry went to his den and hauled the hateful essays out of his briefcase. He looked at the pile, trying to find a title that would suggest some imagination on the part of its author. It wasn't promising. "Sun Imagery in the Poetry of Archibald Lampman" was on top, followed by "Kennedy and Klein, a Study in Opposites." Most of the rest were feminist readings of patriarchal male poets, and of these, about half were attacks on Irving Layton. Near the bottom, however, was one that showed promise. It was entitled "Robert Kroetsch: His Works and the Man Hisself." It turned out to be a brilliant parody of one of Kroetsch's poems. Jerry gave it an F, and wrote at the bottom of the last page, "You were supposed to write a critical paper. Save this for your creative writing class." Its author was Holden Summerfield, a thin, suspicious-looking boy, who missed most of the classes.

For the next couple of hours, he marked a succession of C+s and Bs that could all have been written by the same person. There was no difference in style among them. Finally he picked up Holden Summerfield's paper, stroked out the F and gave him an A without explaining why. There were still a half dozen papers to mark, but he couldn't bring himself to read them.

The hallway was dark, but light shone from under the bathroom door. He opened the door to turn off the light. Inside, Debbie sat naked on the edge of the bathtub. She had painted her toenails red and was waiting for them to dry. Meanwhile, she was combing her dark hair. After the long, dreary haul of the poetry papers, it was too much for Jerry. He scooped her up in his arms, carried her to his bedroom, and dropped her onto the bed.

"Hey, are we really going to go through with this?" she asked.

"You bet," Jerry told her, turning out the light, taking off his clothes and climbing into the bed with her. They made love with all the fierceness that a two-year layoff can generate, and Jerry was exhausted when they were finished. Debbie said nothing, but she lay silently in his arms for a long time after. Finally he told her, "It was a stupid bird. The world is a better place without it." Then he rolled over, and in a couple of minutes he was asleep.

THE NEXT MORNING, DEBBIE was not in the bed. Jerry groaned his way into consciousness with a deep feeling of guilt. He had betrayed someone, only he wasn't sure whom. When he made his way down for breakfast, Debbie was waiting for him, dressed in a dark business suit he didn't recognize.

"Where did you get those clothes?" he asked her.

"They're mine," she said. "I had them with me."

"I thought you only had one pair of jeans?"

"One pair of jeans, and this suit."

"What happened to the pajamas?"

"Well, I didn't think it would be right, after . . . ," and she waved her hand to indicate the events of the previous night. "I mean, everything's different now."

"How is it different?"

"You know?" It was clear that she was not going to be able to explain it to him. "I've got an interview today. I'll probably get the job. I should be out of here by the end of the week."

"You don't have to rush."

"Well, yes, I do. It's not the same anymore. Now if your wife phones making accusations, they're true. So I have to go as soon as possible."

"My ex-wife," Jerry emphasized. Debbie's logic seemed badly flawed, but Jerry couldn't think of just how the fallacy operated. He remembered that in all his dealings with women, a logic that was beyond him seemed to make sense to them. His mother, his wife, his daughters all seemed to work from the same paradoxical premises.

"I'm going to look for a place today," she said. "If I find one, can you lend me the money for the damage deposit? I'll pay you back out of my first cheque."

Jerry agreed because there was nothing else he could do. He looked at Debbie across the table. She seemed like someone he had never met, some distant, formal person who had recently dropped by. He thought about last night's love making, and was struck by a wave of guilt that did not prevent simultaneous arousal. He offered to lend her his car so that she could get around for the day, and she accepted.

He was halfway out to the university by bus before he realized that he had not asked Debbie whether she had a driver's licence or not. He pictured his car destroyed and himself making payments to the crippled couple from the car she had struck. Then he shook his head and remembered why he never took the bus. It made him vaguely queasy, a remnant of the car sickness that had plagued his childhood and was the chief reason his parents never took him on holidays.

He picked up his mail and sorted through it, throwing most of it unopened into the wastebasket in the central office. The basket was already full of other professors' unopened mail. It struck Jerry that it must be possible to develop a mail sorter that could identify publishers' advertisements and catalogues and destroy them at that point, thus saving a number of steps on their voyage to the wastebasket.

"Uh, Doctor King," the receptionist called to him. "There's been a package for you for a couple of weeks. The Rector accidentally picked it up and took it to his office and forgot to return it. He sends you his apologies and hopes it didn't cause any inconvenience."

The package, it turned out when he opened it in his office, was an MA thesis entitled *Elements of the Comic in the Novels of Rudy Wiebe: A Bakhtinian Analysis*. It was written by Marguerite Froese, a Mennonite woman who had taken his poetry class a few years ago and had disapproved of everything he said. She sat tight-lipped and grim, her hair swept back severely, and spoke not a word for the entire year. He had given her a B in the course, which she had appealed on the grounds that all the rest of her university marks were A, and it was clear that it was Jerry who was out of step. He had refused to change the mark, and it had stood.

There was a note from Anderson attached to the thesis. It apologized for the delay in getting the manuscript to him, and reminded him of the date of the defense. Two o'clock that very afternoon. Jerry groaned and stared to read. He liked the novels of Rudy Wiebe, but comic was not the first word that sprang to mind.

The thesis did not disappoint him. It was as long and dull as he expected it to be. Like most successful graduate students, Marguerite Froese had learned the trick of inserting long quotations whenever the argument got complicated, as if the quotations themselves actually addressed the issue. Jerry tried to remember what Bakhtin had said. He hadn't actually read Bakhtin except as quoted in graduate theses, but he thought he had the basic shape of the argument. Marguerite had found a way of combining Bakhtin with Longinus and Edmund Burke in a way which, though thoroughly confused, was certainly original.

The phone rang, and Jerry let the machine answer it. Thelma.

"Jerry, could you please answer the phone?" the voice said reasonably.

Jerry stuck out his tongue.

"Not a chance, you silly old cow," he told the machine.

"All right," Thelma's voice went on. "Take notes because I don't want you to get this wrong. We're going to have a little reunion. The girls are coming home for a weekend very soon and we're all going to get together and talk. There's no room with me and Elena, so everybody's going to come to you, including me. You can sleep on the couch in the rec room. And get rid of the evil, promiscuous teenager you're living with. It's about time you started to grow up."

"I'll burn down the house before I let any of you back in it," Jerry shouted at the telephone, which was now blinking red at him. He thought of Debbie and last night, and was instantly aroused again. Nothing could be more ridiculous, he thought, than a man of fifty, sitting in his office with an erection, reading a thesis on the novels of Rudy Wiebe. And if he were going to get it read before two o'clock, he was going to have to skip lunch.

THERE WAS A MOMENT OF PANIC when he got to the seminar room where the defense was to take place. As the new chair of graduate studies, it was his duty to chair the defense. But since he was also the second reader, he should have found someone else to chair it. The only person around was Sam Baxter, a lanky American draft-dodger, who was never permitted to serve on any committee because his bumbling inefficiency enraged the other members of an English Department already famous for its bumbling. Sam had brought the art of damning with faint praise to new levels, as he demonstrated to Jerry on their way to the seminar room.

"I read your essay in the *Journal of Canadian Fiction*," he said. "I thought a couple of your ideas were really good."

"There are actually three ideas in the paper," Jerry told him with all the sarcasm he could muster. "You must have missed one of them."

"Could be, could be," Sam said. "Anyway, as I said, a couple of them were good."

51

Jerry wondered what the consequences would be if he should suddenly punch Baxter as hard as he could in the side of the head. Baxter was taller, but Jerry would have the advantage of surprise. What would happen, he thought, is the English Department would then join forces with Thelma to have him committed.

At the defense, it turned out that nobody had brought the forms that had to be signed. That was apparently also Jerry's responsibility. He trudged up three floors to the department secretary, got the forms and trudged back down. Baxter was the only member of the department who had memorized all the rules for the conduct of a defense, and he was insisting on them now. Anderson rolled his eyes at Jerry as he entered to indicate that Baxter was well on his way to enraging people. The third member of the committee, the unfortunate, unpromotable Pyncheon from Religious Studies, was staring out the window.

"The student will have fifteen minutes to make her statement," Baxter began. "Then you will each have ten minutes to ask questions. After that, you will each have five minutes to ask any supplementary questions you may have. I will stick to time limits precisely, and cut you off in mid-sentence if necessary. Pyncheon will go first because he is the outside reader. Then King. Finally, Anderson, as the supervisor, will have the last say."

Baxter sounded efficient, but Jerry knew that he would find some way to make the defense a disaster. It was his specialty, turning ordinary events into mayhem. They all agreed beforehand that the thesis was passable but not strong, and that the student would have to put up a good defense or else make significant changes to the manuscript.

Anderson ushered Marguerite into the room. She seemed vulnerable and frightened, not the grim, judgmental monster he remembered from his poetry class. She began her defense in a thin, reedy voice that threatened at any moment to turn into weeping. She argued that until her arrival, Wiebe's work had been seriously misread. He had been seen as making serious examinations of Man's relationship with God and Nature, when in fact that was all parody, and Wiebe was actually a post-modernist who subverted all systems of value. It was, Jerry thought, as perversely wrong a reading of Wiebe as was possible. But, as Anderson continually reminded him, they were not expecting truth. All that was necessary was a coherent and scholarly piece of writing, however wrong-headed it might seem. In twenty years it might be accepted wisdom.

Pyncheon began the questioning with a series of comments on Wiebe's autobiography and his relationship with the church. His ten minutes were nearly up before he finally asked his question: what was the relationship of God to parody? It was an impossible question, but the girl fumbled with it for a couple of minutes until Baxter announced that time was up.

Jerry had serious reservations, not so much about the thesis as about the girl herself. If they passed her and sent her out into the world with a master's degree, she would spend the rest of her life teaching a generation still unborn how to do inane interpretations of English literature. And she was grim enough to fail anybody who tried to speak for common sense.

Still, she was before him, so terrified that her hands shook and her voice broke, and so he decided to ask her something really simple to get her relaxed.

"Could you start by defining for us the term 'Mennipean satire,' as Bakhtin uses it?"

The girl froze. She began slowly to turn red, but she did not say a word. Jerry began again.

"Your thesis uses Bakhtin. The most basic of Bakhtin's

notions is the notion of Mennipean satire. Could you define it for us?"

The girl looked as if she had been stabbed.

"How about 'carnival laughter'? You use the expression at least thirty times in your thesis. Could you define that for us?"

Silence. After a moment Jerry defined the terms himself. He tried asking questions about the plots of the novels, the characters, even their names. The girl had gone rigid and Jerry realized that asking her any more questions would simply amount to cruelty.

"Are you all right?" he asked the girl. Her eyes, fixed on a point on the far wall, did not flicker.

"Time's up," Baxter announced.

"I think maybe this is too trying for Ms Froese," Jerry said. "I think we should give her a few moments to gain her composure."

"If the exam is interrupted it must be rescheduled," Baxter announced with glee. "And the candidate would then not be able to convocate until the next convocation, which is not until May."

With an effort that wrenched her whole body, the girl managed to say, "I'm okay."

Anderson asked his questions masterfully. He began each question with the expression "Would you say . . . ," so that she had only to answer yes or no, and she was able to do that. The second round was only five minutes long, so Pyncheon never actually got around to asking a question. Jerry tried to ask a few more simple things, but she began to tighten and turn red again, so he provided an Anderson "Would you say . . ." question, to which she ungratefully answered no. Anderson declined to ask any more, saying he was satisfied. The girl was sent to Anderson's office to await her fate.

"Well, that's it," Baxter said, unable to hide his delight.

"She's obviously failed. She didn't answer a single question for the whole hour. I don't see how she could pass."

"I don't know," Pyncheon said, staring out the window. "I thought her answer to my first question about God and parody was rather clever. And of course this is a very male-centred experience. I mean, she is being examined entirely by males, and it is not surprising that under these circumstances she might appear a little shy."

Jerry decided that the next time they met, he would vote with the members of the Religious Studies department to deny Pyncheon his promotion.

Anderson twirled his pencil. He clearly did not want Marguerite Froese to fail and come back to him for another year or so. And it was he who had led her to the slaughter, so to speak.

"Perhaps I gave her somewhat leading questions," he said. "But I think by the time she was through she had demonstrated her grasp of the subject."

They all looked at Jerry.

"The decision has to be unanimous," Baxter reminded him. "If one person votes to fail her, then she fails."

Jerry sighed. If anyone had ever failed a thesis oral, this was it. To pass her was to make a farce of the whole proceedings. On the other hand, Anderson would not forgive him if he screwed up his plans. And, in retrospect, the girl's expression might be read not as terrified but as murderous.

"She passes," he told the unbelieving Baxter, and he signed the form in front of him and passed it on to Pyncheon. Anderson brought the girl back, and they all shook her hand and congratulated her. She stared at them with undisguised hatred.

On the way back Anderson gave Jerry a gentle punch in the shoulder and said, "Thanks. I owe you one."

BY THE TIME HE GOT BACK to the office, there was already a message for him from Pyncheon. Jerry called him back. Pyncheon apologized for not talking to him after the defense. He'd had a student coming for a meeting, but the student hadn't turned up.

"I want to clarify what I said at the end there," he said. "When I said that allowances should be made because she's a woman, and that whole oral exam process is a male thing. I don't believe that allowances should be made simply because the candidate is a woman. But the structure brutalizes males as well. Something really has to be done."

Jerry groaned inwardly.

"Look, Pyncheon," he said, "I'm already chairing the graduate committee. I can't take on another committee right now. But if you put together a report recommending changes to the graduate procedures, I'm behind you all the way."

"That's not exactly what I meant," he went on. "Have you read Robert Bly?"

"The American poet?"

"Yes."

"A little." Perhaps a dozen poems in scattered magazines. Jerry had a list of writers he was going to read and another of those he should read but wasn't going to, given the fact that he had but one life to lead. Bly had recently slipped from the first list to the second.

"Do you know *Iron John*?"

"That's the men's movement stuff. Go out and dress in animal skins and howl at the moon?"

"Well, it's been pretty unfairly represented in the media. It's really not like that. A bunch of us get together and talk. It's amazing what a little self-analysis will do for a man. And not to be offensive or anything, but you've had a few difficulties with women yourself lately."

Jerry winced. So he was now an object of coffee-table

chatter. His wife had run off with another woman. It was now two years since she'd gone, but, given the difficulty with which new ideas entered the university, it had only recently become a topic of conversation.

"Thanks," Jerry said, "but I'm really busy these days. Good of you to think of me though."

"I'll send you the book," Pyncheon said, undeterred. "Do read it. It will be good for you."

It was becoming clearer why Pyncheon's colleagues did not want to promote him. Whatever else, tact was not his long suit. Jerry found the remaining six papers he had to mark and hauled them out of his briefcase. It was obvious from the first paragraph of each that it was a C+. Competent, but uninspired. Jerry read several paragraphs of each paper in case inspiration came late, but there was no sign of that in any of them. The second-last page of the final paper was full of glitches. Something must have gone wrong with the computer. First, there were four or five lines of numbers. Then it read, "than in the earlier works where he I love you. Every time I think about yet I get so exciteMany still6403 3578 6742."

Jerry checked the name. Ruth Robataille. He tried to conjure up a mental picture of her but failed. He wasn't vain enough to think the message of love was directed to him. Still, in the middle of an essay on Bliss Carman, it had an oddly erotic feel. She must be the tiny dark-haired girl who sat in the back corner and never talked. Jerry put a large question mark in the margin and left it at that. He put the papers in alphabetic order and started to list the marks. When he got to Ruth Robataille's paper, he read it again, this time all the way through. There were no other messages, but he stroked out the C+ and gave her a B instead.

Evelyn was not in her office, and Jerry judged this a blessing. He didn't know how he was going to deal with her.

She certainly seemed to believe she'd been made love to. Was it kinder to tell her the truth or to let her think that after one free sample he didn't want another? There was no way he could win.

Willie was in her office, down the hall and around the corner. Jerry had no reason to pass by except to go the washroom, and he faked that now. As he passed the door, he noticed that Elena was sitting in a chair, talking in a low, serious voice to Willie. She twirled her walking stick, and Jerry thought he could smell a slight hint of pipe tobacco, though that must be his imagination, because Elena did not smoke.

At the urinal, he brooded on Elena's presence. She and Thelma were inseparable. If Elena were here, then Thelma could not be far away. Still, if Thelma were here, she would have trapped him before now. He had been in his office marking papers, a sitting duck for someone with Thelma's instincts.

When he came back, Elena was leaving Willie's office. She saw him and ducked furtively around the corner and out of sight. Willie had her hair long and brushed so that it seemed to crackle with electricity. She was not wearing glasses, and her eyes seemed slightly red, as if she had been crying.

"Contact lenses," she explained. "A late vanity. I resisted them before, but I thought I'd give them a try. I don't know whether I'm going to be able to wear them." She blinked fiercely, and it made her seem soft and vulnerable.

"What's with the Earl of Dundern?" Jerry asked, indicating the empty chair so recently occupied by Elena.

"She brought me some poems," Willie said, pointing to a manuscript on her desk. "She read them to me aloud."

"Deconstructions of the patriarchal institutions of love or delicate evocations of the tongue? One or the other."

"These are different," Willie said, and she handed him the manuscript.

Jerry read the first few. They were not like Elena at all. They were mournful declarations of passion of the kind written by seventeen-year-old boys, and it was clear that they were directed to Willie.

He handed the poems back to her silently. He didn't know what he could say, so he said nothing.

"Have you read Foucault?" she asked. "*The History of Sexuality?*"

"Yes," Jerry answered. It was true. The only Foucault he had ever read was that precise book, but he had read it.

"Foucault argues that there really is no such thing as homosexuality," Willie said. "He says it comes from the medicalization of pleasure. He says Kraft-Ebbing or Havelock Ellis, somebody like that, invented the term in 1895 to describe an illness. Now psychiatrists have announced that homosexuality is not a medical condition, and so there are no more homosexuals. Only people who choose unusual pleasures."

"Elena would constitute an unusual pleasure," Jerry agreed. "What are you going to do about these?"

"Nothing," Willie said. "I'm going to correct the punctuation and return them."

Jerry took the plunge.

"Are you a lesbian?" he asked.

Willie paused and looked directly at him. "I'm certainly not attracted to Elena, but then I'm not very attracted to most of the men I know. Are you gay?"

"No," Jerry said, recoiling with a little horror. "Why do you ask?"

"Because you asked me. You're not supposed to ask questions like that. You're supposed to figure it out yourself. Those are the rules."

As HE RODE HOME ON THE BUS, Jerry reflected that Willie's answer hadn't told him anything. All that was certain was that if Thelma found out about Elena's infidelity, she was going to be in a rage. And she was going to find some way to understand that he, Jerry, was at fault.

Alf Simmons was sitting in Jerry's driveway on a lawn chair with Rover on a leash. He explained, in a voice quivering with rage, that Rover had dug up his roses again. He had called the pound and had had Rover taken away. Since Jerry had not even noticed that his dog was gone, Alf himself had had to go to the pound and retrieve Rover. The bill was forty-five dollars. He presented it to Jerry. Jerry took out his wallet and counted out forty-five dollars for Alf. Then Alf handed him a brown paper bag. Rover had expressed his gratitude for his rescue by shitting on Alf's lawn. The bag full of shit belonged to Jerry. Every piece of dogshit that appeared on Alf's lawn would be returned to Jerry's without the politeness of the paper bag.

Jerry limped Rover through the garage and out into the back yard, where he chained him to a tree. Debbie was not home. Evelyn phoned and asked him if he wanted to drive out for coffee, but he lied, saying that he was in the middle of marking a batch of papers he had to give back tomorrow, and she was understanding, though there was something in her voice that suggested she would not remain understanding for very long.

Jerry watched television and waited for Debbie. Eastern Europe was in chaos. People were fighting fiercely in countries he had never heard of, equipped with the latest military hardware. How did whole populations who had been docile for a hundred years suddenly find themselves fully armed? He switched from the news to the weather channel. Rain for tomorrow. A chance of thunderstorms tonight. On the music channel, men naked to the waist played guitars while

60

in the background a couple, apparently naked, made love. Rapid cuts prevented the video from actually being pornographic, but as little was left to the imagination as possible.

Finally, just after midnight, he went to bed. Debbie had still not returned and he was worried. She had his car, and he hoped that she hadn't had a burst of wanderlust and left for parts unknown with it. Or been in an accident and destroyed it. He drifted into a fitful sleep.

Jerry woke suddenly to a crack of thunder so loud that it shook the house. Something was clinging to his face, and when he reached out to wipe it away, it was Debbie's hair. He ran his hands over her smooth body, cupped a breast in his hand.

"I got the job," she whispered.

"That's too bad," he said, rolling on top of her. He made fierce love to her, and she responded with tiny cries, finally biting him on the shoulder until he slowed down. Every few seconds, lightning lit up the room as if it were daylight. Then, at the moment of climax, the room stayed dark and the thunder stopped. Jerry heard distinctly the mournful howl of a dog. Rover, still tied to a tree in the back yard.

"Terrific," Debbie murmured, and she rolled herself up in the covers.

"I'll be right back," he told her. His robe was not hanging on the back of the door where he always kept it, so he made his way down the stairs naked. Naked, he went out the back door into the back yard. The door closed behind him with a final click. He twisted the doorknob, but it was too late. He was locked out. Still, it was not a serious problem. Debbie was inside. He untied the dog and took it into the garage.

Then he went back to the door and rang the doorbell. Nothing. He rang again. Still nothing. The storm had renewed its fury. Rain pelted down, cold and stinging on his naked skin. Thunder roared, and so did Jerry. He leaned on the doorbell for what seemed like a very long time, but there was no answer. A car drove slowly down the back lane, and as it passed, lightning lit up the whole neighbourhood, so that he could see the occupants of the car, and was himself exposed to their gaze. Thelma and Elena drove on and disappeared down the lane.

Jerry went back into the garage, out of the rain. Debbie had not locked the car, and the old green blanket he always carried with him in case of emergency was in the trunk. He rolled himself in the blanket and tried to sleep.

THE DOG WOKE HIM. It was whimpering at the car window, standing on its hind legs and looking in. It had apparently been at this for some time, since its toenails had scratched a good part of the paint off the side of the car. He cursed it thoroughly, then walked to the door wrapped in his green blanket and rang the doorbell. Debbie appeared instantly, wearing his robe.

"Where did you go?" she asked. "You disappeared."

"I went out to get the dog," Jerry told her with all the patience he could muster. "It was tied up in the back yard and howling. The door closed behind me and I couldn't get in. I spent the night in the car."

"Well, that's a relief," Debbie said. "I thought you were mad at me because I bit you. I thought you had gone away somewhere. Even though you did deserve to get bit."

"I rang the doorbell a hundred times. I knocked at the door. I shouted at the top of my lungs."

"That's what the noise was. I thought I heard someone trying to break in, and I was frightened because you weren't here. Anyway, I got the job."

"Don't change the subject. I was locked out, and you

refused to let me in. I nearly froze to death. And now I'll probably get pneumonia and die."

"You didn't say where you were going. You didn't say anything. You just got up and left. And I'm not going to bother you much longer. I found an apartment over on Macmillan. I can move in next week. If you lend me the damage deposit. Four hundred dollars."

Jerry didn't know how to respond. On the one hand, he wanted to take her in his arms and hug her and kiss her. On the other hand, he wanted her out of his life as soon as possible.

"How soon do you need it?" he asked her.

"The day I move in."

"Okay," he said. Which was an acknowledgment, but not quite a promise. Maybe he would refuse to give her the money, and she would have to stay with him. He understood that position to be morally corrupt, but he didn't want to dismiss it out of hand.

HE FOUGHT IT OUT TO A DRAW with the Nautilus machine. He hadn't been to the gym for several days, and he was starting to get out of shape, which gave the machine an advantage, but at the same time, he had enough rage built up from his night in the car to offset that.

The dog scratches on the car weren't as bad as he had first thought. He parked in front of the college and rubbed the area with a rag that he kept in his trunk for use at self-serve gas bars. The scratches faded so that you had to look closely to see them.

He threw all his mail in the garbage, unopened. Then on an impulse he retrieved a memo from the Dean. It welcomed him to his new position as chairman of the graduate studies committee, and reminded him of the reports that were missing. His predecessor, Dr. Pickering, an elderly man who lived with his sister and taught Wordsworth and Byron, had apparently given up sending reports to the Dean, which was why they had needed to elect a new chair. Dr. Pickering must have had a first name, but Jerry had never heard it used.

He ignored the blinking red light on his answering machine and phoned Shelley. She was the secretary responsible for the graduate committee.

"How possessive are you?" she asked. An odd question.

"Well, no more than the next man, I guess," he told her.

"No," she said. "I didn't mean that. Dr. Pickering insisted on doing all the paperwork himself. How much do you want to do?"

"None."

"Good. I'll do the paperwork. You talk to people and make the tricky decisions. If the students want to do something that's against the regulations, send them to me."

"I already signed a lot of forms giving people permission to do things that are against the rules."

"I know. And the President's Office is in a snit. Still, it cleared up a backlog, and I can take care of the President's Office. Just don't do it any more."

"You'll do all the paperwork?" Jerry asked. A dream come true.

"Yes. Only don't give me any surprises. If anything complex comes up, say that you have to consult, and I'll take care of it."

"Done," Jerry said, and hung up the phone with delight.

A moment later, just as Jerry had decided that he was going to have to face the answering machine after all, there was a knock on the door. Orest appeared, all six-foot-five of him, rumpled and blond. He sat in the chair across from Jerry, staring at the floor and wringing his enormous hands.

"What can I do for you?" Jerry asked, and Orest turned a deep shade of red. His head was actually the shape of a block. He looked as if he had been hewn from a single tree.

"It's Norma," he said. "The girl I share my office with." He seemed to think that was sufficient information for Jerry to make some sort of decision.

"Yes," Jerry told him. "Go on."

"I can't get any work done."

"What, does she make noise?"

"No, it's not that. It's just . . ." and he drifted off into silence.

Jerry waited. Finally Orest went on. "She won't leave me alone."

"Explain."

Orest turned even redder, if such a thing were possible. "She's very sexually active," he explained.

"Does she bring her lovers to the office?"

"Not them. Me."

"You're involved with this girl?"

Orest nodded his great head.

"Well," Jerry told him, "if you're going to debauch young girls, you're going to have to live with the consequences. What do you expect me to do?"

"She has strange ideas," Orest went on, having broken into confessional mode. "She likes to do it in strange positions. She asks me to do things to her that I can't believe."

"But you do them?"

"Yes."

"Consider it research. You remember your topic?"

"Yes, and that's the other thing. I want to change my topic."

"To what?"

"I don't know."

"How about 'Irony in Robertson Davies'?"

Orest brightened. "Good," he said. "Is that okay?"

"I'll have to consult," Jerry told him. "Come and see me in about a week." He called Shelley and informed her that Orest had recanted and wished to change his topic.

"Anderson is not going to be happy," Shelley said.

"I'm not responsible for Anderson's happiness," Jerry told her. "The world is full of woe." He thought she giggled maliciously at that, but she only said, "I'll let Dave know."

The phone continued to blink red, and reluctantly, he pushed the button. Thelma was first.

"Jerry, you really are insane," she began. "I saw you dancing naked in the back yard last night. I suppose all the neighbours did as well."

"Peeping Tom," Jerry shouted at the phone. "Voyeur."

"You are in serious need of psychiatric help. Don't you understand that?"

"Your habit of blinking," Jerry told the machine. "I could always tell when you were lying because you started to blink."

"I was going to call the police," Thelma went on. "But Elena said maybe you had some things you had to work out. She's really concerned about you."

"You bet she's concerned," Jerry said. "She's concerned that I'll tell you about her little romance on the side."

"It's more than you deserve. But you'd better have a program of rehabilitation in place when the girls come back, or I swear, we are going to have you committed." The sound of a receiver being clunked down decisively echoed in the room.

Jerry thought for a moment, then dialled Thelma's number. Elena answered.

"Look, Elena," he said. "Willie's been telling me that you've been writing some new poetry. I'm putting together a new poetry course for next year, concentrating on women's experience. I wonder if you could send me some of those new poems so that I might consider them for the course."

Elena demurred. The poems weren't ready yet. She was experimenting with a new style. She wasn't sure about them herself.

"Thelma's probably told you," Jerry continued, "about the girls coming for some sort of reunion. They want to use my house, but that causes some difficulty for me. I wonder whether you wouldn't encourage them to stay with you and Thelma."

"There's no room," Elena said. "And I have to work." Elena, Jerry knew, could only write in complete silence. Her muse was diffident and spoke to her only when there was no one else in the house.

"That's too bad. Well, I don't give up easily. I think I'll ask Thelma to get a hold of Willie, and maybe between them they'll convince you to show me the new poems."

"This is blackmail."

"Black phone, I think," Jerry said. "Got to keep up with technological change."

"I'll see what I can do about the girls."

"Good," Jerry said. "I knew I could count on you."

Jerry shifted some papers, and discovered that *Iron John* was on his desk. How it had got there, he had no idea. It was Pyncheon's copy, signed by Robert Bly himself, or at least Bly's name was written on the title page. Inside the book, passages had been underlined in different colours of ink. There were comments in the margin, but fortunately, Pyncheon's hand was so bad that they were nearly illegible. Jerry skimmed through a few sections of the book. It was Jungian stuff, he concluded. He could make out marginal references to The Great Mother, Eliade and Robert Graves in Pyncheon's crabbed hand. He put it in his briefcase to take home that evening. He was pretty sure he was going to despise the book, but there might be some material there for arguments with the feminists.

THE PHONE RANG, and Jerry answered it without thinking. He said hello, then almost hung up before he knew who it was. It was Anderson.

"You got time for a beer?" Anderson asked.

"We can't keep meeting this way," Jerry told him. "People are beginning to talk. What do you want?"

"I'll tell you at Gert's in fifteen minutes," Anderson said.

"Twenty minutes. I've got to go to the can."

"Twenty it is." Anderson hung up before Jerry could make him swear not to mention Heidegger.

It was Edgar Wright who brought up the topic of Heidegger. Edgar was a philosophy professor who was reputed to be the last remaining logical atomist in North America. He was also a paranoid schizophrenic who was normally quiet to the point of timidity as long as he was on his medication. Right now, he was pissing into the urinal and eating a Rice Krispie cake.

"Heidegger," he said, "got it right when he insisted on the difference between *gestunden* and *obzjet*. There is a distinct difference between the chair in which I intend to sit and the merely objective chair that I stumble over on my way to the washroom. Nietzsche said it all in *Beyond Good and Evil* when he distinguished between essence and grammatical agency, though for all that, they both rely on Parmenides, and his notion of things being there in the light." He shook himself and took another bite out of the Rice Krispie cake. "Wouldn't you say?"

"Right," Jerry agreed and he slipped into one of the stalls, hoping that Edgar, if he could no longer see his victim, would assume he had disappeared. But Edgar was not so easily fooled. He went on in a dizzying monologue that evoked Leibnitz, Spinoza and Husserl in aid of a refutation of some position he believed Jerry to hold.

In his depressive stage, Edgar holed himself up in his office in semi-darkness and brought in a string of students who left equally depressed but more fully informed about analytic logic. In his manic stages, he gave up analytic philosophy for continental philosophers and the ancient Greeks, who he appeared to believe were contemporaries. The Philosophy Department was unanimously Analytic in their approach, and believed that any interest in Continental philosophy at all was sufficient reason for commitment to a mental-health institution.

Edgar was in mid-sentence when he suddenly fled the washroom, and the door rattled behind him. A moment later, as Jerry was washing his hands, the Dean burst in.

"Where's Edgar?" he shouted. "I thought I heard him in here."

"Indeed you did," Jerry told him. "Are your intentions toward him as *obzjet* or as *gestunden*, or to put it more clearly, do you seek him as something towards which you have intentions or as a mere object?"

In a second, it was clear that the Dean had intentions toward Edgar.

"He's off his medication," he said. "But I think we've got him trapped. You go through the faculty lounge so that you're on the other side of his office. I'll block off this way. Then we can get him to the hospital."

Jerry was not anxious for a confrontation with Edgar, but he did as the Dean said. Seconds later, Edgar emerged from his office in a parka and a hat with ear flaps. Edgar looked down the hall at the Dean, blocking the escape to the front of the building. He looked at Jerry blocking the escape to the rear, and he made his decision. He turned and came at Jerry, running as fast as he could.

"Get him," the Dean shouted, and Jerry stuck out his arm to stop Edgar. Edgar slowed just long enough to grab the arm and bite it. Jerry shouted in pain, and Edgar galloped past him and down the back stairs, the Dean in hot pursuit.

A human bite is worse than a dog bite, Jerry remembered. He had read that somewhere. The arm of his jacket, where Edgar had bit him, was covered with saliva and bits of Rice Krispie cake, but when he took off the jacket to inspect his wound, he discovered that the skin had not been broken. It was sore as hell anyway.

"IT'S SORE AS HELL ANYWAY," he told Anderson after he had settled into his chair and poured out his tale of woe.

Anderson failed to see the seriousness of the assault. He laughed so much during Jerry's telling of the story that he actually fell from his chair and spilled his beer.

"The stupid thing is," Jerry went on, "that Edgar makes a lot more sense in his manic moments than he does when he's sane. A lot of the time I think I can see what he means."

"Dangerous stuff," Anderson told him. "When madmen make sense to you, you have to ask yourself whether they are actually mad, or whether you yourself are actually sane."

"Thanks."

"You're welcome. But the real reason I invited you here is that other little bit of madness. You know I'm the department's union rep. So I'm looking for people to man the picket lines tomorrow. How would you like to be a captain? Our crew is going to man the south entrance on College Road. What do you say?"

"What are you talking about?"

"The strike. As of midnight tonight we are on strike if there is no agreement. And there are no meetings planned. Ergo, tomorrow morning we will be on strike. Don't you keep track of anything? We voted to strike."

"We always vote to strike. But we never actually strike. How did this happen?"

"The issue is tenure. The administration wants to take away tenure."

"I don't believe it. There are no issues. We don't have issues. Either the Marxists have seized the union or the Fascists have seized the administration, and the strike is based on some lunatic ideology. Which is it?"

"No, Jerry, you have it wrong," Anderson explained, as if he were talking to a child. "The Marxists have always led the union and the Fascists have always controlled the administration. They get along fine as long as there are no issues. But this time there is an issue."

"Well, maybe they're right," Jerry said. "Maybe it's time to get rid of tenure, clear out the deadwood, and make this place something other than a national laughing stock."

"Only they won't clear out the deadwood. The deadwood will stay. Let's try a better metaphor. Think of the university as a broth, and remember that when you're making a broth, the scum floats to the top. If we get rid of tenure, then every real idea in this place, no matter how cleverly disguised, will be rooted out and thrown away."

"That's three metaphors in a single breath. You can lose your licence to teach English for that many metaphors in a row. The strike can't last. This faculty is so lily-livered that they'll all come cringing back as soon as they have to meet their first mortgage payment."

"You'll be surprised," Anderson said. "And speaking of Heidegger . . ."

"Hey, how about them Roughriders," Jerry said. "Thirty seconds to go and they pick up a fumble."

"And miss a field goal."

"Well, hey, it's a start."

BUT THE STRIKE DID GO ON. When Jerry arrived at the university gates the next morning, his way was blocked by a line of picketers carrying signs claiming that the university was unfair and demanding academic freedom. He pulled up at the line and told a balding geologist whom he recognized as one of the regulars at the Club that he just wanted to go to his office and get some papers. The geologist demanded his pass.

"Only scabs go in without passes," he said. "Are you a scab?"

"No."

"Then go on over to headquarters and get one. And you'd better have a good reason. There was plenty of warning. You had lots of time to get anything you really needed."

Jerry did not explain that he had not heard about the strike until last night. Or rather that he had neither listened to, nor believed, any of the strike rumours he had heard. Instead, he backed up and turned around.

He drove for a few minutes, trying desperately to remember where the headquarters might be. Finally, he pulled in at a public phone booth and called Shelley.

"Fabulous Frocks and Sensuous Scents," she told him. "It's in that little mall on the corner of Rockwood and Highway 75. It went out of business a couple of months ago, and the Faculty Union rented it in case of a strike. You have about forty forms you have to sign," she went on in a tone that bordered on accusation. "If you don't sign them, we won't have a graduate program next year."

"That might not be entirely a bad thing," Jerry said. "But how can I sign them? If I cross the picket line, some of the toughs in Human Ecology will beat me to within an inch of my life."

"I'll bring them out after work," Shelley said, "and we can meet somewhere and sign them."

"Where?"

"I'm meeting my boyfriend after work for a beer at the Louis Riel. Join us there at five, and we can do all the paperwork."

"Will I be safe?" Jerry asked. "Do any of those Human Ecology types hang out there?"

"No," Shelley answered. "Only the Chemistry Department, and they're all scabs anyway."

"Will this affect my scabhood?" Jerry asked. "Do I, by signing these forms, enter the brotherhood of scabs, and will I be cast out where there is wailing and gnashing of teeth?"

"I don't know," Shelley said. "That's your problem. I only know that if you don't sign these forms, students who have applied for next year's program will have to go to another university."

"Five o'clock?"

"At the Louie."

"Done."

WHEN JERRY GOT TO STRIKE HEADQUARTERS, the parking lot was full, and the cars spilled over into the empty lot next door. There were half a dozen stores in the mall. But like Fabulous Frocks and Sensuous Scents, most of them were closed and boarded over. Only an optometrist and a Chinese restaurant remained. A large pair of spectacles above the optometrist's sign brooded over the parking lot as if the place had been designed by F. Scott Fitzgerald. The Chinese restaurant was ambiguously named "Frank's."

Inside, the place smelled vaguely like a brothel, or what Jerry imagined a brothel would smell like. Hints of perfume and the smell of new clothes hung, ghost scents, in the heavy air. The place was filled with a sense of excitement, like a theatre moments before the opening of a new play. Along one wall were tables loaded with food, and people were eating meatballs and rice and cold ham and cookies, even though it was only nine o'clock in the morning. A sign above a card table read SIGN IN HERE OR YOU WILL NOT GET STRIKE PAY.

It had not occurred to Jerry that he would get strike pay, and it only now became clear to him that he was not going to get his regular pay. He stood in the line and waited his turn. There were a couple of hundred people in the empty store, in a space that was designed for at most forty. All the professors had dressed down into jeans and old clothes, as if the strike made it necessary for them to declare their solidarity with the proletariat in their very dress. Jerry felt uncomfortable in his jacket and slacks, as if his treacherous and individualist heart was openly revealed.

When he got to the front of the line, the officials, whom Jerry did not recognize, but who recognized him, told him that he was a strike captain, and that he could get his hour's training in a new session beginning in about fifteen minutes. His shift was three to five at the south entrance.

Jerry explained that he needed a pass to get past the picket lines to his office. They pointed out a beefy, red-faced man at a small desk in the corner. He had a computer and a printer, and a sign pinned to his chest that read SYKES, BOTANY, and that must have been left over from some academic conference. Sykes was not very sympathetic to Jerry's request to go in to get some research for a paper he was writing, but when Jerry told him that the main reason he had to go to his office was to get his geranium that would die if he didn't water it, he immediately wrote out a pass. Apparently, the ethics committee had given special permission for people who had to maintain plants or animals that were part of their experiments. Jerry realized that Sykes had misunderstood him, and that he was now the possessor of a fraudulent pass. For a moment he considered explaining things, but he had been at the university long enough to know that explaining anything was likely only to multiply confusion.

"Thanks," he told Sykes, and he folded up the pass and put it in his pocket. Anderson had just entered the room and was waving frantically to him.

THE HALLWAY OF THE COLLEGE was dark and empty. One door was open, and the yellow light spilled out into the darkness. Obermann, Jerry realized at once. Obermann was a sociologist who regularly wrote letters to the newspapers denouncing his colleagues, who, he argued, were filled with nothing but greed and cared not at all for the welfare of their students. Not that Obermann's students were particularly grateful for his interest in them. He regularly received among the worst student evaluations in the entire university. Obermann would not be on strike.

Fortunately, Jerry's office was before Obermann's and he did not have to pass his door. Nevertheless, Jerry took extreme care to be silent as he slipped his key into the lock and opened the door slowly so that it would not creak. The last living leaf on Jerry's geranium had turned black, and it was clear that the plant had no hope for a healthy future, whatever care it was given. He might have to buy a new one and smuggle it in. Jerry didn't know whether the union had a police force that checked out alibis and would come looking for evidence of a live geranium to back up his pass.

The office was a mess. It was no worse a mess than it usually was, but somehow it seemed worse. The constant flow of paper always provided an excuse, but now that the paper had stopped, there was no justification for a mess, and if he stayed in the office, he would have to clean it. The red light on Jerry's answering machine was flashing. Jerry brooded on the problem. If he listened to the messages he would be unable to deny that he had received them. He opened the machine, took out the tape, and turned it over. He left a new message that said "During the strike I will be unreachable. Please do not leave any messages, because I will not listen to them."

Then he turned on his computer and downloaded his e-mail. He had one hundred and forty-seven messages. One hundred and twenty of them were from the same address, and they all invited him to call a special number for free phone sex. He deleted them all with a single stroke, but that still left him with twenty-seven. After the advertisements for printer toner, used equipment, hair restorer and investment advice were removed, he was down to fourteen.

Five were requests for letters of reference. Five were requests for more information on the graduate program, and he forwarded them to Shelley. Two were from Thelma, and he deleted them unread. That left one from the Faculty Union, which gave the address for their Web site, and one from Pyncheon inviting Jerry to join him and a few friends for a "therapy session" on Thursday at seven p.m. at the Madison Curling Club. Howling at the moon, Jerry mentally added to the note, would begin at nine.

THERE WAS NO PLACE TO PARK when Jerry got to the south entrance. In order to discourage student parking, all the streets within six blocks of the entrance were restricted to one-hour parking. It made no sense, Jerry reflected. There were no houses on these streets, no danger to children who might run out from between parked cars. There were no businesses whose clients might need parking space. There were only the fields where neat rows of experimental grains and vegetables were planted by the Faculty of Agriculture. Jerry had never thought about this before. The only reason for restricting parking would be to force the students to pay for parking on campus, where there was not nearly enough space to begin with, or sheer mean-spiritedness, a malicious plan to make the students' lives more difficult. That seemed the likeliest reason.

When Jerry finally got parked and made his way to the picket station, there was quite a crowd gathered. The last shift had not yet left, and Jerry's crew was already there, milling around, pouring themselves cups of coffee and sorting through the Robin's doughnuts to find some that were edible. It appeared that the doughnut bags had been stepped on several times, though they were clearly in the open, and Jerry wondered why. That problem was solved almost immediately. A young man in a red truck opened his window, and when one of the strikers, an elderly woman with silver hair, passed him a pamphlet, he shouted a string of obscenities and roared off, scattering professors like leaves in a fall wind. Two of them leaped back onto the doughnuts. Jerry could see that his first responsible act would have to be to get the doughnuts to higher ground.

Jerry's worst fear had been that Evelyn would be there and that he would have to walk up and down beside her, carrying his sign and explaining his sex life, or lack thereof. Jocko Degraves, a sculptor from the School of Fine Arts, was the out-going captain, and he gave Jerry the special blaze-orange vest that indicated authority and passed him the cell phone. He was to call in at four o'clock to let the planning team know how things were going. He could call in earlier if they ran out of coffee or doughnuts.

Things went on peacefully enough. Jerry knew most of the people on his shift, and they bowed to his authority as if it were somehow merited. There were only two problems during the shift. The first came when Jerry realized that it was four o'clock and time to call in. He picked up the cell phone, which had a lot more buttons than seemed necessary, and he tried to make his call. Nothing. This was not an issue where pride would keep him from asking for help. It turned out, however, that none of the twelve professors there had ever used a cell phone. Even Hawkins, the physicist whom the newspapers interviewed regularly and who was reputed to be at the cutting edge of technology, had to admit that he had never used a cell phone. This was enough for one of the historians to deliver a passionate soliloquy about the defects of the university, his own defects included. He claimed that a sweep of the city could probably not put together twelve people who could not use a cell phone. A few minutes later, the phone began to ring, but nobody knew how to answer it either.

The second problem was more subtle. Jerry had been introduced to one of the members of his crew whom he had not met before, McSweeny from Pharmacy. He had, of course, seen McSweeny. It would have been hard not to see him. McSweeny was well over six feet tall and well over four hundred pounds. He had to turn sideways to go through doors. He was an immaculate dresser who wore brilliant red and yellow silk ties. But he had dressed down for the occasion today. He was wearing a grey sweatsuit with a hooded top, and an old pair of black and white running shoes. The sweatsuit must have been left from the time of a svelter, perhaps a three-hundred-pound, McSweeny, and it opened a large gap between top and bottom that showed about six inches of jiggly flesh.

The convertible Mustang that turned the corner and came toward them belonged to the President's wife, Jerry realized. He had seen it often before. The President's wife, his fourth wife, in fact, was a young woman with flowing black hair, a socialite whose picture often appeared in newspapers and magazines that wanted to add a bit of glamour to the obligatory articles on fund-raising. With her was Allen Green, the arts reporter for a local television station, and in his hand was a camera.

Suddenly, Jerry had a vision of what was going to happen, the sort of vision that people often report having had just before a tornado or an earthquake. He watched in quiet horror as the inevitable unfolded. The car approached the picket line, Green raised his camera to take a shot of the protesting professors, and McSweeny moved towards the doughnuts. Then McSweeny bent over to pick up a doughnut, aiming his vast posterior at the car. His pants slid smoothly over his buttocks and the great gap of his callipygian cleft opened to the oncoming vehicle. The President's wife's mouth opened wide and she made a sort of squeal. Green snapped a shot from his camera, and the flash seemed large even in the brightness of the day.

Jerry could see the headlines already. PROFS MOON PRESIDENT'S WIFE. And he would be to blame. It was on his watch that the disaster had happened. McSweeny was entirely unaware of what had transpired, and he had found a cup of coffee to go with his doughnut. He would be surprised to see so much of his intimate anatomy in the newspapers tomorrow. A few of the others had seen what happened, and now they had gathered around Jerry to ask what he intended to do.

"I don't know," Jerry said. "I don't imagine there's anything we can do."

"Our only chance," said the historian, whose name Jerry now remembered was Carlyle, "is that the photograph will be so horribly obscene that the papers won't dare to publish it for fear of offending community taste."

"Have you seen any newspapers lately?" Jerry asked.

"Right," Carlyle said. "Point well taken."

McSweeny approached them. "Was that Al Green in the car?" he asked.

"Yes"

"That's odd. I was talking to him only yesterday. He was asking me about some new stuff that's supposed to improve male virility."

"Phone him and tell him that you've found it," Jerry said.

"But I haven't."

"It doesn't matter," Jerry said. "Tell him you've got a lead. We can figure out the rest later."

JERRY ARRIVED AT THE LOUIS RIEL BAR in the Saskatchewan Hotel at ten minutes past five. He had passed the bar a thousand times, but he had never gone in. He knew that it was a hangout for the most profoundly alcoholic of the professors at the university. Those who could stay sober until five o'clock and grab a quick beer on the way home met at The Mercury. Those who started serious drinking between two and three in the afternoon met at The Limping Duck. The Louis was reserved for those who began drinking when it opened at eleven o'clock.

It was dark in the bar when Jerry entered, but it was much more cheerful than he had expected. It was all done in bright red vinyl upholstery with a sort of pseudo RCMP decor, hats and boots and crossed sabres on the wall. Apparently the owners of the bar had sided with those who hanged Riel rather than with his supporters. He could smell neither beer nor urine, but only a vaguely lilac odour that drifted from the washroom.

When his eyes became accustomed to the light, he was able to pick out Shelley at a table in the corner. She was seated with a large, beefy man with greying hair who might have been her father. He turned out to be her boyfriend, Al.

"Albert," Shelley said, introducing them.

"You can call me Al," the man said, and Jerry wondered whether he was aware of the reference. Shelley had brought a batch of papers, and Jerry signed them without reading any of them.

JERRY FOUND THAT HE LIKED THE STRIKE. The daily picketing gave an order to his life. His colleagues had never seemed so agreeable. There was none of the rancour or suspicion that he was accustomed to. It turned out that people he knew at a distance also knew him. There was an egalitarian, hail-fellow-well-met air about these professors dressed in ordinary clothes. They were beginning to look like mechanics and carpenters and cooks.

Each morning, he got up late, ate an unhealthy breakfast of bacon and eggs and sauntered down to the gym. His workouts were slower and longer, but he felt better when they were through than he had felt in the anxious, pre-strike days. He had unplugged all the phones in the house, and he had begun to develop the pleasant sensation that he was fully unwanted.

Debbie did not appear at his door, and her complete absence gave her the quality of a pleasant fantasy. Evelyn was on the picket line too, he had been told, but their schedules were different, and the longer he didn't see her, the more unlikely she seemed. He disconnected the doorbell, and when he was home, he watched television in the basement. Only the dog made him vulnerable. It needed to be walked once each day, but it didn't seem to want to be out for longer than it took to complete its toilet.

McSweeny's picture did appear in the paper, but a week later and apparently airbrushed, so that there was only the slightest hint of a callipygian cleft. The picture was grainy, but McSweeney looked enormous, and he appeared to be eating two doughnuts at once. Apparently McSweeney had got through to Al Green, and his vice had been downgraded from obscenity to gluttony.

At the beginning of the fourth week, a snowstorm blew up, with bitter winds and knee-deep snow. There wasn't much need for pickets, since traffic was hardly moving, but Jerry went out and bought a snowmobile suit and rallied his troops. In the two-hour stretch, only three cars passed, and they all stopped and took the pamphlets Jerry was handing out without comment. He had never been happier.

Then one day Jerry arrived at headquarters, and there were only two cars parked in the parking lot. Inside, the scent of perfumed soap that had been masked by the smell of meatballs and sweet and sour spareribs was back. The three people who were shuffling papers at a single desk were surprised to see him.

"The strike is over," they told him. "Didn't someone phone you?"

Jerry felt a surge of irrational anger. Someone might have phoned him, but he had not answered because his phone was unplugged. The news might have been on television, but he had spent the evening watching old *Fawlty Towers* tapes. They might even have rung his disconnected doorbell.

"We're meeting down at the convention centre to vote on the contract. Tonight at eight. Be sure you're there." Jerry was there. He voted against the contract, one of only three who resisted, and he slipped out of the hall and went home.

EDGAR MET JERRY AT THE DOOR of the college the day he returned. November had slipped into December while the strike went on, and Jerry felt as if he had entered a twilight zone and been released back into the ordinary flow of time with something important missing.

Edgar was carrying a placard denouncing the university as a site of apostasy and decay. He was dressed in what appeared to be a mountain-climbing outfit, and it would not have been clear to a passerby just what his complaint was. Jerry nodded hello and tried to slip by, but it was not that easy. Edgar had taken his pickaxe from his belt and was waving it dangerously. He began with a long statement about Parmenides, phenomenology and "being in the light." Jerry tried to object but could only stammer out a series of yesses before Edgar accused him of being trapped in an illusion of Heideggerian auto-affection.

For a moment, Jerry contemplated tackling Edgar and bringing him to the ground. If he acted quickly enough, he might wrest the axe out of Edgar's hands. Then, at the very moment he had decided there was no other course, Robinson, the Associate Dean in charge of undergraduates, appeared, and Edgar abandoned Jerry for larger game. Jerry slipped into the college and peered into the mail room. Evelyn was there, her hands full of mail, and she stared at him coldly.

"Hello, Evelyn," Jerry said. "Did you have an enjoyable strike?"

"Terrific," she said, and she marched past him and disappeared in the mass of students in the hallway.

Jerry felt both guilt and relief. He didn't have to speak to Evelyn at the moment, but he was pretty sure that he would be expected to provide a comprehensive explanation before long. He knew he would have to lie, but he couldn't begin even to shape the kind of lie that would extricate him from Evelyn. He had mountains of mail. His mailbox was full, and so was a large cardboard box with his name on the side in green marker.

He trudged up to his office and poured the mail onto his desk. Then he threw everything that looked like a publisher's advertisement and everything that looked like official university business into the wastebasket. That left a half dozen letters that appeared to be actually directed to him. Five of them were Trojan horses, communications from the Dean's Office that had his name handwritten on the front. The sixth was an actual letter from a graduate student in Edmonton. The student had written a closely argued quarrel with certain claims that Jerry had made in an article about prairie poetry that he had written seventeen years ago. Jerry agreed one hundred percent with the student's argument, but it seemed so momentous a waste of time for anybody to take his statements seriously, particularly at this immense distance from their writing, that he was filled with a momentary despair about the entire academic project. He was about to add the letter to the pile in the wastebasket, but at the last moment decided to reply instead. He pointed out to the student that he had failed to take both Heidegger's *Being and Time* and Nietzsche's *Beyond Good and Evil* into consideration. Then, as a postscript, he added, "Look at Gadamer as well in this respect." That ought to fix him.

He considered calling somebody and reporting Edgar, but decided that the college was a much better place protected by

Edgar at its door than it would be if any passing stranger could enter with impunity. He looked at the bulging wastebasket, and it seemed clear to him that a momentous decision rested there. If he left the communications in the basket, he might as well go immediately to Human Resources and check into early retirement. His arms felt leaden, but he reached into the basket and began to take out the official communications. He answered each of them in order, filling out the forms, writing brief reports and even making a series of telephone calls. Then he looked at each of the publishers' communications, filling out the forms requesting examination copies, and filing the catalogues so that he would have them in March when he filled out the bookstore's requests for course materials.

He carted all the letters down to the mail room, and noticed that Edgar was still guarding the door to the college. Most of the snow had melted, but it was a grey day, and Edgar looked chilly out there. He had put the ear flaps of his cap down.

Jerry deposited the letters in the out box and made his way back to his office. Years ago, he had started a journal in which he had recorded significant events in his teaching career. He picked it from the shelf and read a few entries. They were overwhelmingly pessimistic. The last entry was 1989. He pencilled in the date and wrote, "Today I have decided to seize control of my life."

HIS FIRST ACT AFTER SEIZING CONTROL of his life was to visit his mother. He rang the doorbell and braced himself for the assault on his sanity that he expected. His mother answered the door, subdued and still in her dressing gown, though it was mid-afternoon.

"Oh," she said, her voice full of disappointment. "It's you."

All the explanations Jerry had worked up to clarify why he had not visited her for over a month vanished in his mother's gloom.

"I suppose you'll want coffee," she went on, as if coffee were only one more of the monstrous demands she had to face. "There's some left over from breakfast on the stove. The porridge is cold, but you can eat what's left if you like."

"No thanks." Jerry said. "I had coffee at the college a little while ago. How are you doing?"

"Fine."

"Everything is alright?"

"Just fine." She led the way into the living room. The drapes were closed and the room was lit only by a small lamp in the corner. The remains of several meals were distributed around the room, as if she moved from chair to chair like a visitor at the Mad Hatter's tea party. In all his memory of his mother, Jerry could not recall a single dish going unwashed for more than a half hour after it was used.

"Are you okay?" he asked. "Are you sick?"

"I'm fine," she said. "Just fine."

In the next half hour Jerry tried everything he could to get his mother to reveal the source of her misery, but she maintained her monosyllabic near silence. Finally, in desperation, he asked about Hubert.

"Oh, him," she said. "He's gone. They took him off to the nursing home to die."

"Who took him off?"

"I don't know. The people who do those things. Anyway, he's gone. Good riddance to him."

"I thought he was in perfect health," Jerry said. "He was climbing ladders and painting things only a couple of months ago."

"That's what happens when you get old. One day you're fine, and the next day, poof, the mortuary."

"He's not dead?"

"No. But they took him to the hospital and cut off his prostrate."

"That's prostate," Jerry told her. "They removed his prostate. It's quite common in older men."

"Anyway, they cut off his thingy, and then he wasn't good for anything, so they put him in a nursing home."

"They didn't cut off his thingy," Jerry said. "They removed his prostate gland. The gland is deep inside the body. When men get old, the prostate gland often swells and restricts the urinary tract, and makes it difficult for them to pee."

"Don't talk dirty."

"I'm not talking dirty. I'm explaining how the male body works."

"I know more about how the male body works than I care to," his mother said, but she seemed to have brightened a bit. "Is that why he took so long in the bathroom?"

"Yes," Jerry said. "That's probably the reason."

"Doesn't matter," his mother said, suddenly gloomy again. "He's got prostrate cancer. He'll be dead in a week."

It slowly dawned on Jerry that his mother might be mourning Hubert. In spite of her long war with him, she probably missed him.

"Prostate," he said. "Prostate cancer. And at his age, it's not going to kill him. Something else will get him first. All it means is that he probably won't have much of a sex life from now on. But he should be fine."

His mother brightened noticeably.

"You think he won't die?"

"Everybody dies, but I think he's probably got a few years left in him."

"Then why did they put him in the nursing home?"

"Probably so that there would be someone to take care of him. Probably he realized that he couldn't take care of himself any more, and he went of his own accord."

Jerry's mother was suddenly galvanized into action.

"Pick up those dishes," she told him, "and carry them into the kitchen sink. They're disgusting." She said "disgusting" in a tone of voice that suggested that Jerry was responsible for the mess. "I'll wash them and you can vacuum. You never used to clean your own room like your sister Carol. I don't know why I used to put up with it."

Jerry vacuumed. He washed windows, and repaired and puttied a missing pane. He repaired the Adirondack chair on the back deck. It was getting dark when he said he'd have to leave. His mother presented him with a cardboard box full of his childhood toys, mostly stuffed animals and toy trucks that had stood on the dresser in his bedroom since he had left home thirty years ago.

"No use keeping these around," she said. "You may as well have them."

"I don't want them," Jerry said. "Give them to the Salvation Army."

"They're your toys," his mother said with relentless logic. "You give them to the Salvation Army." And so he packed them up and took them home. He didn't know what to do with them when he got home, and so he put them up in his bedroom, just as they had been in his mother's house.

The next morning, the phone rang at six-thirty, and Jerry was awakened from a dream of sexual fulfillment so real that he resisted consciousness until the phone had rung at least a dozen times.

"I've got him," his mother said, her voice full of triumph. "He's sleeping in your bedroom right now."

"What are you talking about?" Jerry asked, though he already suspected the answer.

"Hubert," his mother told him. "I rescued him from the nursing home."

"What did you do?"

"I went there last night, right at midnight. I marched into his room, packed his bags, and took him home. We caught the last bus from the west end, and I carried the bags all by myself."

"And now he's sleeping in my bedroom?"

"Yes."

"Does anybody know you did this?"

"No," his mother said. "That's the best part. Nobody knows where he is, so they can't come and take him back."

"Mother, that's kidnapping. You can go to jail for that."

"Go to jail for helping a poor old man with nobody to care for him? This is a fine country, isn't it? We might as well be living in Russia. Well, I've got him now, and I'm not giving him back." And she slammed down the receiver with a noise that told Jerry he would not be forgiven if he called the police.

CHRISTMAS WAS COMING. The exam period had begun, and suddenly the hallways were empty. Whatever students were around had found vacant classrooms and were studying in them. Many of the classrooms looked like shelters for the survivors of some major disaster, a flood or a hurricane or a civil war. Plates were piled high on the tables and clothes were flung haphazardly around the room. In some classrooms, there were even sleeping bags, pillows and suitcases. The smell of stale pizza spread out into the hallways. Cautionary notes forbidding food in classrooms and reminding students that the rooms and the building would be locked at ten p.m. were taped to every door, but it appeared that while the college had the legislative power to make the rules and the judicial power to create imaginative penalties, it lacked the executive power to carry out any of its threats, and the notices were universally ignored.

It was Jerry's favourite time of year. He told Anderson over beer at Gert's that the university would be a wonderful place if it could be freed of students. If the mail could be stopped and all the telephones removed, it would be perfect.

"What you are looking for is a monastery," Anderson told him. "There are several you can join if you are really serious. How are you at making cheese?"

Jerry confessed that he had never made cheese. He thought he could handle a vow of silence if necessary, but he had very little talent for gardening.

"Too bad," Anderson told him. "Several members of the English Department have ended up in monasteries. Remember O'Brien? He ended up as a gardener in Scotland. And Big Ed O'Malley? He's a monk in Saskatchewan. And the American. Lindmann? Liscomb? He's now a hermit somewhere in the Rockies."

"So a PhD in English is practically a prerequisite?"

"Well, some form of religious faith is usually helpful, though probably not essential."

"No good," Jerry told him. "I couldn't fake it. I was removed from the Christmas pageant in grade two for spreading apostasy among the members of the nativity scene. I apparently told Joseph and Mary that God was dead, and it brought them to such a point of crisis that neither one could remember his lines. Or her lines as the case may be. Have you seen Evelyn?"

"She's in the hospital. Been there for over a week. You mean you haven't been to see her?"

"What is she doing in the hospital?" For a moment Jerry had the feeling that she had done this deliberately, taken a room in the hospital and not told him in order to ratchet up his guilt.

"They don't know. They're doing tests. She collapsed at Faculty Council the last day of classes. You don't need to go into a monastery. You manage to be a hermit quite well right here."

"How did she collapse? Was there shrieking and waving of arms? Was there blood? Or did she just faint gently to the floor?"

"A gentle faint. She slumped in her chair, and nobody even noticed until the meeting was over and almost everyone was gone. It was the Dean who noticed her."

"I'll have to go see her. I'll have to send her flowers. Did the department send her flowers?"

"I sent her flowers in the department's name. Did you know that the university has a policy not to send flowers? They keep sending us invitations to contribute to the fund-raising drive, but they will not send flowers for our graves if we die."

"That can't be."

"Scout's honour. No flowers under any circumstances. Direct orders of the President."

EVELYN WAS ASLEEP in the hospital bed when Jerry arrived. The room was filled with flowers, and Evelyn was propped up in her bed, her eyes closed and breathing lightly. She looked like an illustration from a nineteenth-century anthology. Last photo of a dead poetess.

"Jerry," she said, opening her eyes. "How good of you to come. You must be terribly busy, what with Christmas coming on and all. Are you expecting the girls home for Christmas?"

Her words struck Jerry like a blow. Of course the girls would come home for Christmas. Thelma would have thought of that. She had missed October, but Christmas would be perfect. Gather everyone when he would have no chance to escape.

"I hope so," Jerry said, feeling the insincerity in his own voice. "They said something about a reunion. But I don't know for sure. Nobody has confirmed."

"Elena and Thelma were by. They said that the girls were coming. Apparently they invited the girls to stay with them, but the girls have insisted on staying with you."

"That will be nice."

No amount of questioning could get Evelyn to admit what was wrong with her. She was even vague about the symptoms. They were doing tests, but she seemed unclear about what sort of tests these could be. When Jerry left the hospital, he was as unclear about her condition as when he had entered. On the brighter side, she was no longer overtly angry at him, and treated him as a somewhat distant acquaintance, for which he was grateful.

WHEN JERRY ARRIVED AT HIS HOUSE, he found an enormous black Ford Expedition with Alberta plates parked in his driveway. His Mazda Miata looked like a toy beside it. The back of the Ford was filled with leather things, saddles and harnesses and what appeared to be the sort of chaps that cowboys wore in the comic books of Jerry's youth.

Inside, the house smelled sharply of disinfectant, with the slightest overtone of manure and something else, and there were fragments of straw on the mat at the door. The television was running somewhere, and from the sound of it, a football game was in progress.

"Hi, Dad," Cindy called from the kitchen. The something else that Jerry had smelled turned out to be beans cooking on the stove. Cindy was stirring them as Jerry entered the room. Her blonde hair had been permed so that it covered her head in tight curls. She was wearing jeans and a checked shirt. Her face was tanned, and she looked fit and muscular, though she had not gone to fat as he had suspected she would.

"You've got it all wrong," he told her, giving her a fatherly hug. "The costume is right, the perm, the jeans, the checked shirt, even the ruddy glow, but the weight is all wrong. You'll have to put on another forty pounds to look proper-ly rural, or Pete will chuck you for a more substantial woman. You don't look as if you could pull a plow for more than half a day." He took the wooden spoon from her hands, and stirred the beans a couple of rounds. "But I suppose if you keep it up with the beans, that will all come in time. Where's Pete?"

"Pete's in the rec room watching the football game. And you can lay off with the sarcasm for a minute. Life is not one of your novels where people go around speaking in *bon mots* all the time. Can't we be serious for a few seconds?"

"If it wasn't for me you wouldn't even know what a *bon mot* was," Jerry countered. "You'd think it was a kind of exotic French chocolate." He passed her back the wooden spoon. "No, no, I couldn't handle another *bon mot*. I'm on a very strict diet. But I would like to try one of those *je ne sais quoi*s."

"That kind of talk could get you into serious trouble in a bar in Alberta," Cindy said.

"With any luck, a merciful providence will save me that dubious pleasure. My idea of hell is a bar in Alberta where you have to listen to k.d. lang on the jukebox, and go line dancing with three-hundred-pound women who stomp on your toes for fun."

Jerry noticed that every surface in the kitchen had been polished until it gleamed, a clear rebuke of his own house-keeping. The refrigerator was stocked with skim milk, non-fat cottage cheese, natural peanut butter, margarine and hordes of green leafy things. A bowl of fruit on the table dribbled grapes and bananas over its edge.

"Anyway, let's not get into a fight within minutes of meeting. Lise and Leon are flying in this afternoon from BC. They're landing in some farmer's field south of the city, and we're going to pick them up."

"Just any old farmer's field?" Jerry asked. "Can you do that? Aren't there laws about private property?"

"It belongs to a friend of Leon's dad. He has his own landing strip and a hangar where Leon can leave the plane. They sent us a map."

Cindy handed Jerry the map, which looked more like the outline for a scavenger hunt than anything seriously intended to get you to a particular place.

"I think it's a map of Egypt," Jerry said. "See, here's the Nile, and over there is the Red Sea."

"Pete will figure it out. He's good at maps. Why don't you go in and talk to him? And by the way, you'll have to go out to the airport and pick up Margaret. She's flying in from Minneapolis."

"Minneapolis?"

"She was at a conference in Philadelphia. Didn't Mom explain all this to you?"

"She didn't mention a word. I suppose she wanted it to be a surprise. I guess you've ruined it now by telling me."

"Well, you knew we were coming soon. I told you that myself."

"Yes, you did," Jerry said. "Only I didn't expect it so soon, what with the harvest and the round-up and all that, and Christmas nearly on us."

"Go talk to Pete. Supper will be ready in a few minutes. We're having falafels."

"Of course," Jerry answered. "I suppose they don't allow those in Alberta. Effeminate things made out of beans."

Cindy didn't rise to the bait, so Jerry moved on into the family room where Pete was staring morosely at the television.

"Hi, Jerry," Pete said without turning to look at him.

"Ah," Jerry said, seating himself on a chair near Pete. "The Grey Cup."

"The Grey Cup was three weeks ago."

"So who is playing?"

"The Bears and the Patriots."

"Never heard of them. Must be eastern teams."

"You have so heard of them. Every human being alive on this continent has heard of them. It's American football."

"Oh, well," Jerry said. "I never watch that foreign stuff. How's Alberta?"

Pete gave up hope that he was going to be allowed to watch the end of the game in peace and turned to Jerry. He was an enormous man, starting to get a belly that promised similar proportions, and Jerry realized that the diet food in the kitchen was aimed at Pete and not at him. Pete had a large bald spot, his moustache was tinged with grey and his bright blue eyes looked startled in his leathery face.

"Alberta is doing just fine," Pete said. "Though I can't say the same for the rest of the country."

The temptation to enter into political debate was nearly too much for Jerry. Pete was an active member of the Reform Party, and Jerry had teased him about his wild-eyed optimism the last time they met. Cindy had been outraged at Jerry's behaviour. Pete was a good man, she had told him, and Jerry could keep his professor's tricks of argument to himself. With a tinge of regret, Jerry allowed the opportunity to slip.

"You're looking good," Jerry said. "Out in all kinds of weather, hard work, the simple life. Keeps a man in proper shape. Now me, pushing a desk all day, it's hard to keep from turning into a marshmallow."

Pete was not fooled. He knew of Jerry's workout regimen.

"You're in pretty good shape yourself. Ranching is hard work all right, but there are rewards. Cindy and me are taking off a month in February and spending it down in Texas, right on the Gulf of Mexico."

"How long have you and Cindy been together now?" Jerry asked.

"Five years last month."

"Was there something you wanted to tell me?"

"No. What are you talking about?"

"Well, I don't know anything for sure, but I noticed as I came in that she was thickening a little around the waist. Might be nothing, but I wouldn't mind a little grandson."

"What? Did Cindy tell you . . ."

"No, no. Just father's intuition. I know you'll do the right thing by her."

"What are you talking about?"

"Well, it's just that it's tough for a kid to grow up, well, you know, being called names."

"It's Cindy who doesn't want to get married, not me." Pete had stood up from his chair and drawn himself up to his full size as if he were ready to fight. "She's the one who doesn't want a bourgeois arrangement."

"Of course," Jerry said. And just then Cindy called them for supper. As they walked into the kitchen, Jerry whispered to Pete, "I know when the time comes you'll do the decent thing." Pete took his seat at the table in a murderous calm.

MARGARET'S PLANE WAS LATE. Jerry walked into the airport bar where a few lonesome travellers sat alone nursing drinks. He was tempted to join them and nurse a Scotch for the forty-five minutes that he was going to have to wait, but he thought better of it. He'd had two glasses of wine with supper, and he did not want to take the chance of being stopped by the police and breathalyzed. His life was sufficiently complicated without being conducted entirely on foot.

Instead, he bought a newspaper and sat down to read it. He had let his subscription lapse after Thelma left and found that he did not miss it. Now he was appalled by what he read. Everywhere there was war, accidents, violent deaths and corrupt and venal governments. His own miseries seemed trivial in comparison. He had not read a paper for two years, and he remembered now the daily sense of dismay he had felt, reading it in the old days. Yet almost everyone he knew read it thoroughly every day. What was it doing to their minds?

When Margaret's plane finally arrived, Jerry had lapsed into a partial coma waiting for her to clear customs. Almost all the other passengers had left and the waiting area was nearly clear when she finally arrived in a towering rage.

"They ripped through my suitcase," she reported. "The filthy swine pawed through my clothes and thumped the suitcase and brought dogs in to sniff it. They left me waiting by myself for about an hour, and then they went through their little charade. Meanwhile, a hundred real smugglers probably got through because they were dressed like business men. But no! They stop me! Do I look like a smuggler?"

Margaret was dressed in jeans and a tee-shirt under an old, ripped jean jacket. She was carrying a small backpack and wearing round glasses that made Jerry think of John Lennon. She had her hair wrapped in a red polka-dot kerchief that reminded him of one that Marilyn Monroe had worn in some ancient photo. She looked exactly like what Jerry imagined a smuggler would look like, and he knew that if he were a customs officer he would have investigated her bag.

"No, honey," he said. "You look very beautiful. You look like a famous movie actress in disguise."

"Is that sarcasm? I hope it isn't sarcasm, because I've had a terrible trip and I don't think I'm up to much sarcasm."

"No," Jerry said, and it was true. He had not intended to be sarcastic. "You look very beautiful, but you do look like someone who has dressed down for the occasion. Customs officers go to movies. That's where they learn to look for what is suspicious. They only went through your bags because that's what customs officers do in movies when a beautiful woman dressed in jeans tries to slip into the country. Are you sure you aren't a spy?"

"Right. A spy from New Brunswick."

"Well, we don't know that. We have only rumours that you are living in New Brunswick, no hard evidence like a letter or even a postcard."

"Nobody send letters or postcards any more. I phone, but you never answer your phone. I send you e-mail, but you never answer your e-mail."

"I forgot my password," Jerry answered in his defense. "I wrote it down somewhere but I lost the piece of paper it is written on."

"So somewhere in the bowels of the university computer there are hundreds of e-mails waiting for you. And you are going to have to answer them sometime. It's only going to get worse."

"You can't hit a moving target," Jerry said. "It's my philosophy of life." It was actually Anderson who had accused him of living by that philosophy, but he had so liked the idea that he had claimed it as his own. He gave Margaret a gentle peck on the cheek, picked up her bag and headed out into the prairie night, where the snow had begun to fall in big, fat flakes.

LISE MET THEM AT THE DOOR, delivered Jerry a fat, sloppy kiss, and hugged Margaret.

"How are you guys?" she asked, as if Jerry and Margaret had a single history and either could answer for the other.

"Great," Jerry said. "Top of the world."

"Lousy," Margaret added. "About the worst trip I've ever had. It was more like a roller coaster than an airplane. And we sat on the runway in Minneapolis for over an hour for what the pilot called minor repairs. They could have replaced the entire engine in that time."

"Anyway, sweep the snow off and come on in. I've made a pot of chili." Lise was even smaller than Jerry remembered. She could not have been much over five feet and she weighed about a hundred pounds. He remembered teasing her when she was young that she was a changeling, that his real baby had been stolen by elves, and she was the elf baby that had been left behind.

"I hate chili," Jerry told her. "I've always hated chili, especially Mexican chili. The better it is, the less I like it. Surely you remember that."

"I also remember I have never seen you even taste it. I don't think you know what it tastes like. You had it once as a child and have steadfastly refused it ever since. You are going to love it."

Lise was right, Jerry admitted to himself. He could not remember when he had last tasted chili. He had eaten all of the ingredients in other dishes, and loathed them individually, so he didn't see how this combination was likely to thrill him. Still, he took direction and ate the chili, and was surprised to find that he didn't mind it. He even had another helping, which pleased Lise out of all proportion to her victory.

Pete put away a cowboy's portion, but Leon didn't finish his small bowl. Leon was as tall as Lise was short. He had to duck his head coming through the doorway from the family room into the kitchen. He had a long, skeletal face that made him look even taller, and big hands with long fingers. Although he didn't wear glasses, he looked as if he should have been wearing aviator lenses and a leather World War II pilot's helmet. Jerry's daughters had apparently chosen perfect stereotypes. Both men looked exactly like what they were supposed to look like. A cowboy and a pilot. Later that evening, just as Jerry left for bed, Pete took out his guitar and started to sing Ian Tyson songs. Jerry had seen him look toward the case standing in the corner and made his move fast so that he didn't have to listen for an hour out of politeness.

Big day at the university tomorrow, he told them. And a long meeting of the fund-raising committee in the evening, so he wouldn't be home for supper. It was all a lie. He had no classes, and no meeting. He wasn't sure what he would do, but he was certain that he did not want to spend a family evening with his daughters after they had spent a day deciding what was to be done about him.

THE LIGHT ON HIS ANSWERING MACHINE was blinking when Jerry arrived at his office. The first message was from Edgar. It accused him of the naïvest form of auto-affection, and explained at some length the difference between Hegelian and Marxist dialectics. It very nearly made sense, and Jerry almost re-played it before he realized that it was a short journey from the ordinary life of a professor to Edgar-style madness, and it was a journey he would sooner not take.

The second message was from Evelyn. She had something she wanted to talk to Jerry about. Could he meet for lunch at The Club? She'd be there at noon and hoped Jerry could come. Jerry was surprised that she was back from the hospital and in action so soon. There was nothing on his calendar for lunch that day. In fact, there was nothing on his calendar at all, he hoped, though he would have to call Shelley to see whether some disaster had happened to his little flock of graduate students.

The third was from Thelma. The girls would be going out to a restaurant with her for dinner. If Jerry wished to join them, he could. Six o'clock at the Thai Palace on Jerome Street. Come or not, as he liked, it was up to him. Jerry restrained himself from insulting the answering machine, and he realized that it was the first time he had managed that. A small victory, perhaps, but if he was going to have to meet with Thelma and all his daughters, he had better get in practice.

The final message was from his mother. Hubert was doing fine. They hadn't fed him properly at the home, but she was fattening him up. The police had come to her door asking whether she had seen Hubert. They told her that he had Alzheimer's and had wandered away from the nursing home. They thought he might appear at his own house. She had promised to phone if she saw him. She appeared to think that it was terribly funny. Jerry envisioned a future in which he drove out to the prison every second day to visit his mother, and thought that a responsible son would inform the police and get his mother proper psychiatric care. Maybe he would do that early in the new year.

He called Shelley. She had arranged one meeting for him. Orest Ryhorchuk had something urgent to discuss. She had set up the meeting at eleven-thirty at the department seminar room. She also informed him that he was supervising an exam at one o'clock. He had completely forgotten. It had been twenty years since he had forgotten to go to an exam, but he still remembered the experience of explaining

David Arnason

his absence to the Dean as if he were a delinquent child. That Dean was long since dead, but the memory of it was as intense as if it had happened yesterday.

OREST INFORMED HIM THAT he was getting married. He and Norma Jean were tying the knot on December 31, New Year's Eve, in order to get the tax break. Jerry was invited to the wedding.

"It's unusual to marry for the tax breaks rather than for mundane things like love," Jerry told him, "but then, you probably move in higher financial circles than a mere university professor."

"No," Orest told him, he did love Norma Jean, but it was his dad who had told him to do it before the end of the tax year.

"So you've resolved your problems," Jerry said. "You are no longer finding the athletic rigours of the relationship too strenuous?"

"Well, actually not exactly," Orest said. It was his dad again. He had brought up the problem with his father, who had told him the simplest way of shutting down a woman's sexual appetite was to marry her. And actually, since they had got engaged it was a lot better. Norma Jean was so busy preparing for the wedding that she didn't have much time for him. And also, she wanted Jerry to know that she had decided to do her thesis on the Renaissance. Dr. Chamberlain had agreed, and the defense was scheduled for the first week in January.

"Good," Jerry said. "But what about the novel?"

"She says she hadn't realized how incredibly dull the life of a football player was. She said nobody would read the novel, so what's the point?"

"Good thinking. And how's Robertson Davies going?"

"Well, actually that's why I'm here. I'm going to drop out of the program."

"Why, is old Robbie too dull for you?"

"Well no, or actually, yes, I hate the books, but that's not the reason I'm quitting. It's just that, being married and all, we've got to buy a car and a house and furniture and everything, and I think maybe I'm not really cut out to be an English professor."

"Don't be too hasty. A lot of English professors are failed engineers and failed architects and failed artists. Why not a failed football player?"

"Well, Norma Jean is going to teach. I don't know if you know it, but she has a teaching certificate. She's got a job at a First Nations school."

"An Indian reserve?"

"They call them First Nations now."

"And you are going to go out into the frozen north and be a househusband?"

"No. I've got a job. I'm going to Germany to play hockey."

"I thought you were a football player."

"I am. But also a hockey player. They pay a lot in Germany, and you don't actually have to be very good."

"It seems an ideal way to start a marriage. One of you in an isolated reserve in the north, and the other living the high life in Berlin. I don't see how it can fail."

"It's only for a couple of years. Until we get enough money to buy a car and put a down payment on a house."

"The time will fly by," Jerry said. "You may expect me at the wedding, complete with fish slice and silver bowl."

"You don't have to buy a present."

"Oh, but I will," Jerry said, rising and herding Orest in the direction of the door. "I want to."

THE CLUB HAD BEEN THE FACULTY CLUB in palmier days, but it had nearly gone bankrupt until someone had decided that changing the name to The Club and inviting anyone who wanted to join, including students, might save it. And whoever had made the decision had been right. The Faculty Club had been a dreary place, where the most seriously alcoholic members of the Faculty of Agriculture and the Departments of Physics and Chemistry had gathered to debate rightwing politics and play pool in the afternoons, and a dartplaying contingent of British professors in exile gathered in the evening. Lunch had rotated from roast beef on Mondays to fish Fridays with an execrable lasagna on Wednesdays. Nobody had been able to get the menu changed, even with almost unanimous petitions and a total boycott of the lasagna.

Now, the ambience had changed considerably. The place was all gleaming stainless steel, specializing in salads and middle-east vegetarian plates. The old pool players and dart throwers had retired to The Limping Duck, where the introduction of strippers had reduced their athletic interests, though not their thirst. The Club was now full all the time with a more casually elegant clientele, mostly young people from the high-tech business park on the edge of the university. Enough ferocious, overweight, white-bearded professors still decorated the odd table to lend the place ambience, but not enough to give it the whiff of death that had doomed the Faculty Club.

Evelyn was already at a table by the windows when Jerry arrived. She was gazing out the window, looking pale and thin, like the heroine of a nineteenth-century novel. He waved to her, then made his way down the salad bar, rejecting all the items that were swimming in oil or laden with mayonnaise. That left him with a plate piled high with lettuce and melons, the fruit salad having lost all of its more expensive items to a recent cold wave in Florida.

"How is family life?" was Evelyn's first question.

"Just like the old days," Jerry replied. "The place smells like a brothel, except for the odd whiff of manure from the cowboy and the smell of gasoline from the pilot. The dog, however, is in his glory. He hasn't had his belly scratched so much since he was a pup."

"Is Thelma spending the time with you as well?"

"Thelma?"

"I thought perhaps you two had reconciled."

"I think not. Thelma has made it perfectly clear that she believes that I would rank on the food scale between the slug and the larva beetle. Given half a chance, she would grind me mercilessly beneath her heel."

"You haven't heard? Thelma and Elena have had a falling out. They are no longer *simpático*."

"French," Jerry said. "French is the only foreign language you are permitted to bring into our conversations. What are you talking about?"

Evelyn gestured with her arm and Jerry followed until his eyes settled on Elena at a table with Willie. They seemed in deep conversation, oblivious to all around them. Jerry's heart sank. He was surprised at his own dismay. He had thought that he would feel nothing but glee at the news of the failure of his wife's relationship, but now it seemed somehow both tragic and seedy at the same time.

"Willie?"

"That's the scuttlebutt."

"How is it that everybody alive knows things before me? Is there a conspiracy to keep me in the dark about the workings of the world?"

"Other people live in the real world. Other people sometimes think about something other than themselves."

Jerry was suddenly filled with a sort of hopeless anger, the kind of anger that sometimes struck him when he read about large injustices in the world, wars and famines and ugly violent coups, things about which he could do nothing. At that moment, Evelyn seemed somehow responsible for the ills of the world.

It was a moment of decision.

"Evelyn," Jerry said, gathering his energy for a momentous statement, though he still wasn't sure what he was going to say. "There's something I have to say to you."

"It will have to wait. I want you, for once, to listen to what I say, and to pay attention. This is not an opportunity for a great one-liner."

Jerry looked directly at Evelyn, meeting her watery blue eyes under her pale eyelashes.

"When I was in the hospital, I had a lot of time to think, and I didn't always think nice thoughts. The doctors told me I have cancer. It's a slow-moving cancer, but it will kill me as surely as any other cancer. I have a fixed amount of time left in this world, and I intend to live that time, not to waste it waiting for some great event to occur. Do you get what I mean?"

Jerry waited.

Evelyn took a deep breath. "I mean you. I am no longer interested in waiting while you sort out your problems. They are nothing I can help you with, though Lord knows you need help. In other words, I will greet you as a colleague, and I will work with you on any committees to which we are both named, but I am no longer interested in having you as a friend or anything more than that. It is simply not worth the effort."

Jerry realized that he had been given the gate. He had been out-manoeuvred once again. He realized that he should be exultant, but he wasn't. He looked over to Willie at the table with Elena. Strike one. He looked back to Evelyn. Strike two.

"Now you wanted to tell me something?"

"Orest," Jerry said. "Orest has dropped out of the program. He is going to Germany to play hockey." His response sounded lame and unlikely, even to Jerry, but it seemed to satisfy Evelyn. She nodded, excused herself, and prepared to leave. Jerry had asked her a little more about her cancer, but she remained mysterious. It was something she had to work out herself, and she really didn't want to talk about it. Did he mind?

Jerry was certain that Evelyn did not have cancer. It was simply another attention-getting ploy. He was sure that it was somehow aimed at complicating his life, but the moment he thought that, he realized that it was an ungenerous thought, and he remembered Evelyn's accusation that he thought about nothing but himself, and wondered if it might not be true.

He looked over to Willie and Elena. They were still in deep conversation. Then, beyond them, a massive figure shifted in his chair. McSweeny from Pharmacy, he of the callipygian cleft. To McSweeny's left was Jocko Degraves, looking like the figure Pan from a Grecian urn, and Al Green, who looked far more athletic and several years younger than he did on television. With them was a stunning young woman in a business suit. She was leaning over and apparently whispering something in Al Green's ear.

Jerry moved in their direction, thinking vaguely that he might make some gentle reference to their strikers' days when the woman looked at him and laughed. It was Debbie. Jerry shifted direction, thinking he might escape, but he had come too far and too decisively. Degraves waved him over and there was nothing he could do.

They all looked at him as he approached. McSweeny lifted his giant head from his heaping plate, then tucked back into the roast beef. Al Green whispered something to Debbie and she laughed again.

"Want you to meet some friends," Jocko said. Jerry had marvelled for several years about Degrave's ability to speak whole paragraphs in which no sentence had a subject. "Working on a project. Shake up this university. Al Green. Works at CBC."

Jerry nodded in Green's direction.

"I like your movie reviews," Jerry said. "I never actually go to movies, but I listen to you describe them, and then I don't feel guilty about not going."

"And Deborah. Deborah Van Heusen. Business gal extraordinaire."

"Hi, Jerry. How's Rover?"

"In the lap of luxury. Petted and spoiled. Fed on honeydews and the milk of paradise. Bathed in rosemary and scented with frankincense and myrrh." He realized that he had been speaking in fragmented sentences, as if he were parodying Degraves, so he went on. "The slavering beast filled with blood lust that you grew to know and love has been transformed by the love of a good woman. Three good women, in fact."

"Margaret? Is Margaret home? I'll have to give her a call."

"You two know each other?" Green asked. His name had been linked with many of the beautiful women in the city, and the present rumour was that he was a bit too cosy with the President's wife, another hangover from the strike. As a famous seducer, he ranked right up there with Jocko Degraves, though he specialized in the wives of the rich and well connected, while Jocko made do with graduate students and the wives of professors. They seemed to have found a common interest in Deborah.

"I'm a friend of Jerry's daughter," Deborah said, a trifle ingenuously, Jerry thought. "Jerry was very kind to me when I first came to the city."

"It's a friendly city," Green said. "People will do anything for you. Anything at all." It seemed clear that his words had some other meaning. And Debbie's response showed clearly that she had caught whatever secret they contained. Jerry was suddenly filled with a fierce jealousy and a sense of his own impotence. Why hadn't he looked Debbie up? Why hadn't he called her? He had allowed her to walk right out of his life, and now it seemed clear that she was filling her life with other people.

"Be careful," Jerry told her. "You've fallen in with bad company."

"Don't I know it," she answered, and she gave him a wink that was clearly lascivious and produced a huge guffaw from Degraves.

"Bad company," he said, nearly choking on his steak. Green toyed with his salad, and Jerry noted with satisfaction that he had spilled a drop of oil on his silk tie.

"Well, see you," Jerry said and left the room without turning around, as if to look back would doom him to exclusion. "Strike three," he whispered to himself. "Three strikes and you're out."

JERRY CALLED HIS MOTHER, breaking his own private rule of never calling anyone on his own initiative. A small notice on page four of the newspaper pointed out that an Alzheimer's patient from a nursing home who had walked away was still missing. The police still had no information, but Jerry suspected that before long they would. How long could you hide a person in your house without someone catching on?

"He's fine," Jerry's mother told him. "He doesn't get around too well, so I have to practically carry him from chair to chair." Jerry had a momentary fear that Hubert was dead, and his mother was lugging the body around the room like a large decoration.

"He is alive?" Jerry said, half a statement and half a question.

"What are you talking about? Of course he's alive. He eats like a horse, and he talks non-stop. If he's dead, he's the liveliest corpse I've ever seen. It's just he's got arthritis. Lots of pain. You don't happen to have any prednisone lying around?"

"Mother, you are not going to medicate him on your own. You are not a doctor. You can go to jail for giving wrong medication to people."

"If I'm going to jail for saving him from the nursing home, what does it matter if I also go to jail for medicating him? We had some prednisone left over from your dad's arthritis, and it made Hubert feel a lot better. But I'm almost out. Maybe I can get some from Dorothy. Her husband had arthritis, and she probably has some left."

"Dorothy? Dorothy Parker?" Dorothy and Alf Parker had lived across the street for years, but, as far as Jerry knew, his mother and Dorothy had an ancient blood feud that had something to do with one or the other's cats shitting in flower beds. "Alf isn't even dead."

"That's where you're wrong, mister smartypants. Alf died yesterday. I saw the ambulance take him away."

"Maybe you ought to wait a couple of days before you borrow his unused medicine."

"No. I have to bake some cookies and take them over for her anyway. I'll just go into the bathroom and take it out of the medicine chest. She'll never know, and it will be one less thing for her to throw away. That's the toughest part. Throwing things away."

"Mom, you never threw anything away. You still have all Dad's stuff."

"See what I mean?" she said triumphantly. "It's no easy chore."

Jerry held the receiver in his hand for a long time, debating whether he should call the police. No, he concluded. A man who turns his own mother in to the police is the most despicable of all creatures. Though that was apparently a class to which he already belonged.

Someone knocked on the door. Pyncheon. With him was Ronald, the fat political scientist from next door. Ronald had a big voice, and Jerry could often hear him through the wall talking on his telephone. His favourite expression was "pas de sweat," a phrase that had turned Jerry even more fiercely against the French language with all its affectations, though maybe it served French right that it should be mangled in Ronald's mouth.

"Tonight at seven," Pyncheon said. He handed Jerry a sheet of paper on which he had scratched a map. It appeared to be an identical map to the one that led to Leon's airplane.

"Thanks," Jerry said, putting the map into his pocket. "What happened to the Madison Curling Club?"

"They're using it for curling."

"You weren't evicted for rowdiness?"

"No."

"Well, I can't promise, but I just may see you there."

When Jerry walked into the Limp Biscuit to meet Anderson, an entirely naked woman was dancing on a small stage surrounded by tables. She was very small and extremely pretty, and Jerry had a feeling he had met her somewhere before. Perhaps she had once been one of his students. Jerry was accustomed to meeting and failing to recognize ex-students. Usually men who had been thin and intense had become pot-bellied, balding and garrulous. Women who had looked like budding fashion models were mysteriously transformed into cranky mothers who didn't take care of themselves. They all spoke to him with a world-weary cynicism, and Jerry wondered whether this was their customary pose, or an attitude they adopted in the presence of their ex-professors.

Anderson was already there by himself in a far corner with a mug of dark beer and a bowl of popcorn. He waved to Jerry and craned to see the dancer who was now lying on the floor and visible only to those in the front row.

"Julia Helmsholm," Anderson explained, indicating the dancer. "MA in Philosophy. You were the outside reader, remember?" Jerry did indeed remember. He had agreed to sit as external reader on the basis of having minored in philosophy as an undergraduate. He had been chosen reluctantly by the Philosophy Department as a sort of last resort, every other professor in Arts having turned down the opportunity to read a huge work on the philosophical implications of artificial intelligence. They had turned to Jerry in preference to exploring candidates in agriculture and geology.

Jerry had accepted in a weak moment of collegiality and immediately regretted it. He had been sure that philosophy, at least, would not change. It had been there for several thousand years. Aristotle was surely the same Aristotle he had been in Jerry's earlier encounters with him.

It turned out that philosophy had indeed changed. He could make no sense at all of the thesis. He had never even heard the names of any of the sources to which the thesis referred. About halfway through, he came to the nagging suspicion that the thesis did not in fact mean anything, that it was not intended to mean anything. It had a curious kind of bullying logic to it, but none of the conclusions made any sense at all. At the defense, Jerry was prepared to point out the sheer obfuscatory language of the thesis, but the philosophers on the committee were so mean-spirited and aggressive that he found himself on the candidate's side, if merely on the general principle of supporting the underdog. When it was over, he assumed that he would be the sole vote in favour of passing her, but as soon as she had left the room, the philosophers pronounced the thesis a work of genius, worthy of publication. They called her back, congratulated her in a perfunctory manner and left.

Jerry was in the awkward position of having to speak to her, and, since he knew nothing of the philosophy in which she had specialized, he mentioned Nietzsche to her. She had apparently never heard of Nietzsche or of Hegel for that matter. She had a passing knowledge of Plato and Aristotle, and had heard of Kant, though she had not read him. Jerry encouraged her to read Nietzsche and warned her away from Hegel. That was the last time he had seen her.

"Is this the usual career path of Philosophy MAs?" he asked Anderson.

"Well, males usually go into bee-keeping, but ecdysiasis is a not unusual course for a young woman."

"More critical theory? Let me guess. Roland Barthes?"

"H.L. Mencken. An ecdysiast is a stripper."

"And speaking of the university," Jerry said, though they had not been speaking of the university, "do you know that a certain blockhead has decided to marry, then abandon his bride to the wilderness and move to Germany?"

"Orest. Yes. I had high hopes for Orest, but you win a few, lose a few."

"Orest may not be a significant loss."

"Anyway, Orest and his ilk may soon be somebody else's problem. There's a move to dethrone you. The Commander has taken umbrage with your running of the graduate program. There's a special meeting of the graduate committee to discuss your handling of several delicate cases. In particular, your handling of Darwin Case."

Jerry tried to bring an image of Darwin Case into his mind, but failed.

"I'm sorry. Darwin Case?"

"You flunked him out of the program. He was the Commander's pride and joy. He was going to write the definitive study of early nineteenth-century detective fiction, and now he faces a lifetime as a publisher's representative, endlessly knocking on professors' doors and trying to get them to buy hateful books of poetry and critical theory. And meanwhile, early nineteenth-century detective fiction goes scandalously unexamined."

Jerry remembered. "Case? He's the guy who failed his comprehensives?"

"The very one."

"I didn't fail him. I wasn't on the committee. I didn't even chair the oral that failed him. I haven't met him. I haven't even seen his file."

"So you admit all the charges? Your defalcations as graduate chair have been responsible for Case's downfall. And you would have let him slip away unnoticed."

"That's ridiculous. Nobody in his right mind could hold me responsible for Case's failure."

"We are speaking of the Commander here."

"Yes, of course. I forgot. So what do I do?"

"Go to the meeting. Explain your side of the story. Confess the error of your ways. Promise to do better in the future."

"And you think the committee would support me?"

"Yes. The Case case really is ridiculous. The committee, in spite of all your fears, will actually do the right thing."

"In that case, there is no chance of my attending the meeting. I seek nothing more than my own defrocking or dethroning, or whatever it is that happens to disgraced committee chairs. To you from failing hands I throw the gavel. Be yours to hold it high."

"Just go and explain. Case was so dumb that he made even Orest seem like a genius. I was on the committee that failed him. He couldn't answer any of the questions."

"Since when has that been a problem? Most of the questions make no sense and the answers bear no relationship to the questions. Case was around long enough. He attended the exam. He should have passed. The Commander is right. I should never have signed the form failing him, and if I had read it, I would not have done so. I'll have to take my punishment."

"Come to the meeting."

"Not a chance. I will hereafter devote myself to teaching, which is my first love, and you will have to take over the administration."

"That is exactly what will happen. I'll get the grad committee along with all the other committees I chair. Be a sport. The Commander is miffed, but he'll see reason. And I need help."

"Hey, how about them Roughriders," Jerry said.

"I don't want to talk about the Roughriders."

"What about Heidegger? Let's talk about auto-affection, or even better, thrownness. *Dasein. Being in Time.*"

"Those are topics on which you have no information."

"Hey, I'm better than average. At least I know they're topics."

Just then, a strong whiff of perfume signalled the arrival of a young woman in a silk Japanese kimono.

"Hi, Julia," Anderson said. "You remember Dr. King?"

"How could I forget the man who introduced me to Nietzsche? How's it going, Dr. King?"

"Terrific," Jerry said. "Couldn't be better."

Julia took a seat and put down her glass of soda water. "One more set," she told Anderson. "Lulu didn't turn up, so we've each got to do an extra set."

"Fine," Anderson said. "No rush."

"Did you pick up groceries?"

"Everything but oven cleaner. They were out of oven cleaner."

"They were not out of oven cleaner. They are never out of oven cleaner. You looked in the wrong place."

Jerry felt a strong sense of the surreal. The conversation had become domestic so quickly that there was no room for misunderstanding.

"So you two . . .," he began, then hesitated.

"What?" Julia said. "You bring your friend to watch me strip and you don't even tell him we live together? You're disgusting."

"I'm not supposed to tell anybody. Remember? That's the agreement. I don't tell anybody. And besides, Jerry didn't watch. He's much too much the puritan to watch a stripper."

At that moment, Jocko Degraves came through the door with Debbie. They took a table near the stage, and Jocko waved to the waiter to bring them beer.

"I've got to go," Jerry said. "I'm late for an appointment."

"Think it over," Anderson said. "Go to that meeting. If nobody stands up for reason around here, the place will sink into a hellhole of incompetence."

"Sure," Jerry said. "I'll think."

Debbie got up and went into the women's washroom. Jerry tried to get by without being noticed, but Degraves called out his name in a loud voice, and Jerry went over to the table. Degraves was wearing a leather jacket, and though it was December, he appeared to be wearing a Hawaiian shirt beneath it. He wore a heavy gold wedding ring.

"Grab a seat, join us for a second. Debbie has been talking about you. A little worried about you. Thinks you might not be taking care of yourself."

"I'm fine. Tell her I'm fine." Jerry said. "I've got to go. I'm late for an appointment."

"She's quite a gal," Degraves said, swinging his head to indicate the door to the women's room behind which Debbie had recently disappeared. "Quite a gal." He gave Jerry a long, obscene wink.

"Yes," Jerry said. "You've hit the nail on the head. Quite a gal. Look, I've got to run," and he made his way past the drinkers craning their heads to see the dancer and offended by his momentary blocking of their line of vision, out into the darkening night. The phrase "fled from the scene" echoed in his head, and he tried to drown it out by playing the radio in his car as loudly as he could. How long had Anderson had this domestic arrangement? Anderson never talked about his private life, and Jerry realized he had never asked. He had assumed that Anderson had a suburban wife somewhere and probably a couple of kids.

He was at the edge of the city before he realized that he only needed to keep driving in the direction he was going to follow the map that Pyncheon had drawn for him. A left turn at River Road then another at Borden and he was there.

The music stopped, and the news reported unrest in countries that Jerry knew he would never see. The world was filled with land mines and ambushes. Just like his life, Jerry thought, a series of land mines and ambushes. Then a familiar voice began to talk about a new movie playing at the Garrick Theatre. Al Green doing his weekly radio review. The movie he was reviewing was a flop, and he recommended that the audience avoid it like the plague. Apparently it was a story about a sexually frustrated and incompetent professor who gets himself into a series of unfunny situations and has no resources to extricate himself. Green had watched half of the movie, then walked out.

Right, Jerry thought. Ambushed again. Only this was his life, and however much he wanted to, he was not going to be allowed to walk out halfway through.

SNOW HAD BEGUN TO FALL in large flakes by the time Jerry reached Borden Road and turned left. Roads led off into the whiteness, but there were no numbers by the roads, and it was impossible to see what was at the end of the driveways. He stopped and parked the Mazda on the road where a bunch of other cars were parked, and walked down a driveway that led into the swirling blackness.

After a short walk, Jerry made out a large black shape in front of him in the driveway. The shape turned out to be a black Ford Expedition with Alberta licence plates. It looked like Pete's vehicle, but the licence plates were no guarantee. In oil-rich Alberta, probably everybody drove Ford Expeditions. The large house to his left was completely dark, but he could see a light in the window of a building a little further on. He followed a pathway to the door of the building and was about to knock when he realized that he might be in entirely the wrong place. Instead, he stomped through the deeper snow to the window and peered in.

The place seemed to have once been a barn, because there were stables and harnesses hanging from posts, but there were no animals. A large fire burned in a wood stove with an open door, a sort of homemade fireplace fashioned out of an old forty-five-gallon drum. A dozen men sat in chairs or lounged on piles of blankets around the fire. Jerry recognized Pyncheon and Ronald, his neighbour of the big voice, but the rest of the men were strangers to him. A man in some sort of paramilitary costume was speaking to the group. He was holding a gun, which he was taking apart in an obviously professional manner.

The men in the group watched the speaker in rapt fascination. Jerry noticed that all of them were dressed in some form of animal skin. They wore leather or sheepskin jackets and vests. All of them were in jeans, and all of them wore cowboy boots. They looked like a posse getting their instructions from the sheriff before driving the rustlers out of town. Jerry realized that in that scenario, he was the villain. The outsider peering through the window. The man in the uniform reassembled his rifle in a few quick moves, loaded it and pointed it directly at the window through which Jerry peered. Jerry ducked, then felt a hand on his shoulder. He whirled, falling into the snowbank and managing a stifled scream of the kind that signals a nightmare, but quite loud enough, he thought, to bring out the posse.

Instead, hands picked him out of the snow and helped him to dust himself off. At that close range he was able to recognize Pete and Leon.

"What are you doing here?" Leon asked. "Did the girls send you?"

At first Jerry missed Leon's point. Why would the girls have sent him out to meet Pyncheon and his band of gun fanciers? He soon realized that Leon had assumed that he was in search of them.

"No," he said. "I was supposed to meet some people. I'm not even sure that this is the right place."

"If it's those guys," Pete said, indicating with a gesture the men in the barn, "they're a mighty strange crew. A few minutes ago they were out in the snow, singing and doing some strange sort of dance. At first I thought they were drunk, but there doesn't seem to be a six-pack among them. I suppose they're professors?"

"No," Jerry said. "They're just a bunch of guys." Then, in a moment of inspiration, he added, "They're a hunting club. They get together for male bonding, tell a few stories, a few lies. They all go down to the pub for beer after the meeting."

"You got some strange friends," Pete said. "I recognize that survivalist guy, the guy in the funny uniform? He's from around Pincher Creek. He's famous for firing off a few rounds at the Mounties whenever they go near his place."

"They're not really friends," Jerry said. "More like acquaintances. They invited me to this meeting because of something I wrote. I don't actually know any of them. But what about you guys? What brings you here in the dead of night?"

Jerry was pretty sure he didn't have to ask the question. They were out there because Leon was worried about his plane.

"I was worried about the plane," Leon said. "And Pete drove me out. We stopped for a couple of beers on the way and kind of lost track of time. The women are going to be frantic if we don't get back. You driving the Mazda?"

"Yes."

"You want us to wait and follow you? The snow's getting pretty deep."

"No," Jerry said. "I've got to at least make an appearance. Besides, you'd better get back to the women. Hell hath no fury, you know."

"Yeah," Pete agreed. "Don't we all know it."

Pete and Leon trudged back to the Expedition. Jerry intended to wait a decent amount of time and then follow. He would leave Pyncheon and his fellows to their ceremony. But just as Pete and Leon got into the truck, the door behind him opened and Pyncheon appeared in the orange light.

"King? Is that you?"

"Yes," Jerry said. "It's me."

"Come on in," Pyncheon said. "It's cold out there. We thought we heard voices."

"Yes, well, I was talking to a couple of guys who happened by."

"The cowboy and the fly guy? They're strange. Who in his right mind goes out flying in weather like this?"

"I don't think they were flying," Jerry said. "I think they were just checking their airplane."

"They were flying all right," Ronald added. He had just stepped out through the door. "And drunk as farts. They buzzed the barn here a couple of times, and we couldn't hear ourselves think."

"We thought they might be going to commit suicide by crashing into the barn," one of the sheepskins added. By now, Jerry had been ushered into the barn, and he could feel the heat from the fire. The guy in the uniform had added another log, and the sides of the barrel gleamed a dangerous red. "They must be absolutely crazy."

"This is Jerry King," Pyncheon said to the group in general. "His wife left him for another woman, and he's got a lot of issues he has to work out."

"Not really," Jerry said. "The marriage was over anyway. Doesn't much matter what happens after that."

"Don't worry," said another man in sheepskin. "Happens to the best of us. It's a new world. Women have found a new place for themselves, and more power to them. But it's time for us to reclaim a space for ourselves."

Suddenly, Jerry felt an overwhelming need for a drink. He didn't want to enter this discussion, but the others seemed determined that he should. "We've got to reclaim a space for male desire. The male gaze does not limit women. It expands men." The man who offered this looked like a member of the Classics Department, but by the time the introductions were over, he revealed himself as a pharmacist.

"Depression is entirely chemical," he told Jerry. "Don't let your therapist put you through any of those talking cures."

"I don't have a therapist," Jerry said. "I don't need a therapist."

"Right on," the survivalist, who was named Maguire, agreed. "They'll try to get you onto some loony doctor's couch, then they'll use that to take you for everything you've got." His demonstration was clearly over, but he kept disassembling and reassembling the rifle with lightning speed, and apparently without even looking at it.

"Look," Jerry said. "I've had a rough day. You guys don't happen to have a beer?"

The group in general had lost interest in Jerry and had begun to discuss the gun laws, which they appeared to believe were intended solely to emasculate men. He overheard someone say, "Next thing you're going to need a licence for your penis. Probably charge by the inch."

"No," Pyncheon said. "No alcohol. Another device for enslaving men. Have a couple of beers, forget about your troubles. Slave all day for your family and drop drugged into bed. We've got to get out of the cycle of violence and dependency. Face our troubles in the stark light of day."

It did, in fact, seem brighter in the room, and Jerry soon realized why. Flames had started to lick up the post with the harness on it, and had already spread to the hay in the empty stable beyond the post. He was apparently the only one to notice it.

"Fire," he shouted, and he lunged for the door. He had at that moment the answer to a question that had troubled him since a course in philosophy in his first year at university. He would not lie to prevent panic. Instead he would panic himself and shout "Fire."

The others seemed in some sort of denial. Several of them continued their conversations as if nothing had happened. The others took off their coats and tried to beat out the flames. Maguire, the survivalist, showed his credentials by getting out of the building almost as fast as Jerry. The flames rose, and Pyncheon's crew filed out of the building one by one. The pharmacist had a cell phone, and he dialled emergency and the police, but there was no answer, nor was there any answer when he called his wife.

"The wind must have blown down the tower," he

announced, and he headed for his car, parked on the road. Pyncheon offered Jerry a ride, which he refused, then he and the others departed, leaving Jerry and Maguire to watch the flames, which by now had burned through the roof.

"It's a pretty sight," Maguire said, taking a mickey of Five-Star whiskey out his pocket and offering it to Jerry. Jerry took a pull from the bottle and returned it. Maguire wiped the top of the bottle with his sleeve and took another deep pull. For several minutes they passed it back and forth, until it was empty. Then Maguire dug down into the snow at the foot of a nearby tree and returned with another. They continued to drink and watch the flames. Jerry began to be filled with a sense of deep bonhomie. Maguire was a decent sort, a generous and sharing man.

"Too bad the others had to leave," Jerry said. "It's such a lovely fire."

"Bunch of wusses," Maguire said. "Bunch of goddamn sissies." He had taken off his jacket and was warming himself at the fire, which by now had begun to burn itself out.

"Right," Jerry agreed. "Bunch of goddamn wusses."

JERRY WOKE TO THE SMELL OF BACON and eggs, and stumbled to the shower. He could hear music playing, then the sound of a radio voice, slow with the exaggerated rhythms of a news report. At least nobody had tried to claim his room. He still had the sanctity of that. The water turned cold about a minute into his shower, and Jerry cut it short. He would have liked to make the water hot and stand with his head directly under the flow. Over the years, he had found that he was able to lift everything from his mind in that simple way. Instead, he had a sudden and unwelcome vision of himself and Maguire dancing before a fire in the blinding snow. He could not, however, remember how he had got home and into his own bed.

Everybody was at the table when he arrived, and the breakfast seemed pretty well over. Margaret offered to fry him up some more bacon and eggs. But Jerry opted for a lone grapefruit. He planned to enter combat with the Nautilus machine again. It had been weeks since he had done any exercise, and he could feel that he was becoming flabby. Last night's excursion had taught him just how badly out of shape he had become.

"We had supper with Mom last night," Cindy said. "You should have been there."

"No," Jerry said, "I don't think I would have been a great asset. And I had a meeting at the university, you remember?"

"What was the meeting about?" Pete asked, then, aware that his question might be perceived as treachery, added, "not that it would make much difference to me."

"It was the Shirks," Jerry said. "We were doing the ranking. We have to do it every year at this time."

"Isn't it late?" Margaret asked. "Don't you usually do that in October?"

"Only in the East," Jerry told her. "Here in the West we do it a different way. How was your mother?"

"Not very good," Lise told him. "She's pretty unhappy. Things haven't been going very well for her."

"She's resilient," Jerry said. "I'm sure she'll pull through."

His daughters looked at each other. It was clear that they had cooked up some sort of plan.

"Dad," Margaret began. "Do you think you could find time for a cup of coffee sometime today?"

"Sure," Jerry said. "As a matter of fact, I am drinking a cup of coffee this very moment, but I'm sure I'll find the time for another cup sometime later."

"Could you meet me for a cup of coffee?"

"That's a different question. I've got a very busy day."

"Make time. How about 2:30 at Mario's?"

Mario's was an Italian café in the trendy shopping district downtown. Jerry had been there once before and found the place depressing, filled with what would have been boulevardiers had this been Paris.

"Will I have to wear a scarf and a beret?" he asked.

"Be serious."

"Yes. Yes, of course. I will be there, and fully serious."

"Good."

THE ANSWERING MACHINE WAS FLASHING its red light when Jerry got to his office. He reached for the button that would launch it into speech, but the telephone rang before he could press it. It was his sister, Carol, calling from Montreal.

"Jerry," she began, "this is Carol. You can answer the phone if you are there. This is important." She paused.

Jerry answered the phone. "Hello, hello, hello," he began, and breathed heavily as if he had made a dash to catch the message.

"It's you," Carol said. "In person?"

"Yes," Jerry answered. "You are incredibly fortunate. I was just leaving to go to a meeting."

"Do you actually go to meetings?"

"Not if I can avoid them. But this one I can't avoid."

"Well, I called to give you my big news. Bob and I are moving back. Bob has been given a promotion. He's going to be in charge of the whole western area."

Jerry had never been quite sure of what Bob actually did for a living. He was somehow involved with the Department of National Defense in a civilian role, and he had titles like Director of Operations. He was an engineer who had taken an MBA at Western, and so he might have done anything from building runways to buying tanks.

"That's great," Jerry said. "Just great. When does this happen?"

"Right away. Bob has to start the first of January. We'll all be there for Christmas, then Bob will stay with the kids, and I'll go back to Montreal to sell the house and make final arrangements. I guess we'll stay with Mom for a few days until we find a place."

Jerry realized that some of his chickens had come home to roost. He should have told Carol about his mother, consulted with her on what to do about their mother's criminal tendencies. He was going to have to tell her now.

"That's probably not a good idea, Carol," he said. "You'd probably be better off in a hotel. Won't the government pay for a hotel?"

"Yes, of course. But Mom has lots of space, and I'd like the kids to get a chance to know her."

Jerry was pretty sure that his mother was not going to bond with his sister's children, however optimistic his sister.

"Well, she actually doesn't have all that much room. She's sort of taken on a boarder."

"She doesn't have to take in boarders. She has enough money. What kind of boarder?"

"Remember Hubert next door? Him."

"She told me the last time I phoned that he was in a nursing home. She seemed depressed. Actually, she hasn't answered any of my messages for over a month. Is she all right?"

Jerry decided to come clean. He explained how their mother had captured Hubert and how she was now secreting him in her house and repelling all boarders. He tried to make his reactions seem caring about their communal mother, but he realized quickly that he was not convincing Carol. She had always been stone-hearted and relentlessly practical. He had never understood why men were attracted to her. Even as a young woman she had seemed formidable.

"Jerry," she asked, "is this sheer incompetence on your part, or is it lunacy?"

"Ninety percent incompetence, eight percent carelessness and only two percent lunacy."

"You really should be locked up."

"That appears to be the prevailing opinion around here. I have a houseful of ungrateful daughters with their aging, slothful husbands, a madwoman of a wife who is out to get me for everything I've got and a flea-bitten dog ready for the mortuary. Mother is yours. To you from failing hands, and all that. You call the police on your own mother and visit her in the penitentiary. I'm going to run away from home."

"Oh. And where will you go?"

"Australia," Jerry said. "Tasmania. That's where criminals go to start a new life. I need a new life." Suddenly, the idea of Australia seemed very appealing. It was always warm there. Palm trees and surf and lovely beaches. Through his window, Jerry could see that it was snowing again. Snow was piled high along the sidewalk, and he could see the toques and scarves of passers-by, hidden beyond the drifts. He thought of waterfalls and kangaroos and crocodiles. Australia!

"Grow up," Carol told him. "That's my advice to you."

"I think it's bad advice," Jerry said. "I've seen some grown-ups and it's not a pretty sight. Bald heads, halitosis, Parkinson's disease, rattling teacups in wheelchairs."

"We get in on Christmas Eve. Can you meet us at the airport?"

"I have a Mazda Miata. A two-seater. There isn't even room for you, much less Bob and your herd of progeny."

"We have three kids. Hardly a herd. And we don't have to

ride with you. We can take a cab. But it would be nice to have someone meet us when we arrived. Isn't that what family is all about?"

Jerry was not sure quite what family was all about, but he agreed to meet her anyway.

JERRY BUMPED INTO ANDERSON at the bookstore. Anderson was browsing the Critical Theory section of the reference works. He appeared to be debating whether or not to buy a large book with the name Derrida on the cover.

"Don't," Jerry said, taking the book from Anderson's hand and replacing it on the shelf. "It will only confuse you and take bread from the hungry mouths you must feed."

"Oh, hello, King," Anderson said, picking up the book again and putting it under his arm, confirming his intent to purchase. "Did you get home alright?"

"It's a long story," Jerry told him. "And why did you keep it secret that you are in residence with the beautiful Ms Helmsholm?"

"I assumed you knew. It was the scandal of the Arts Faculty a mere two years ago. I am a confirmed moral degenerate, co-habiting with a woman young enough to be my daughter. I assumed your failure to bring the matter up was a sign of your inherent delicacy and tolerance. Now I find it was only insularity. King, I am disappointed."

"I register no disapproval. Moral degeneracy is fine with me. I see you have been unable to convince her to give up her profession?"

"I have made no attempt to do so. Ms Helmsholm is saving her money to buy a villa in France. It is her hope that I will take early retirement, and that we will spend the rest of our lives eating baguettes and drinking *vin de pays*. Besides, it's your fault, or rather Nietzsche's fault."

"How is that?"

"It's a question of agency. Nietzsche says that the wolf does not choose to eat lambs. To be a wolf is to be an eater of lambs. In the same way, to be Julia Helmsholm is to be a stripper. She likes the work. The hours are short, the pay is good, it keeps you in shape. And it's portable. Naked women are everywhere in demand. Even in France."

"Is that why you didn't get the headship? Moral turpitude?"

"No, moral turpitude can be forgiven in a head of department, may even be a requirement. It was the critical theory that did me in. I had been seen smuggling books about semiotics and deconstruction and hermeneutics into my office. It was rumoured that I encouraged helpless students to read Deleuze and Guattari."

"Well, of course, that's true. You have been warping young minds."

"Yes, it's a curse, but I can't seem to give it up. It won't be a problem for long, though. Julia has earned far more than I ever believed possible. We'll be moving to France a year from July."

"Truth?"

"Scout's honour."

Jerry brooded about Anderson on his way back to his office. He didn't believe for a moment that Anderson would actually leave, but he found the fantasy of a life of leisure in France attractive. Except for the weather. Jerry and Thelma had spent part of a sabbatical in a little town north of Paris, and it had rained every day for the three months they were there. Or that was what Jerry remembered. They had lived in a tiny apartment and the girls had been cranky and sick and nobody understood Jerry's French, even though he had passed the reading exam for his PhD. Thelma remembered it as the best part of their marriage, and the more he thought about it, the more he was convinced that she was right.

Back at his office, he found a note taped to his door. It contained only a phone number. Jerry threw the note into the basket, retrieved it, threw it back into the basket and retrieved it again. He was certain that it would be Pyncheon with an explanation about the fire, but when he dialled the number, Debbie answered.

"Who's calling?" she asked in her distracted voice.

"It's me," Jerry said. "Your ex-landlord."

"Oh Jerry," she said, and he could imagine her face brightening. "What can I do for you?"

"You taped your phone number on my door."

"Oh, right. I have to talk to you about something. Can you meet me for coffee this afternoon?"

"No. Not this afternoon. I'm meeting Margaret for coffee this afternoon."

"Oh," she said. "Where?"

"It's a secret. Downtown."

"Well, I have to talk to you."

"Tomorrow? Ten in the morning? At the Java Shoppe?"

"I've got to work in the morning. Big meetings. How about two o'clock?"

"Fine. See you then."

There were shouts in the hallway, angry voices, and the fire alarm began to ring. Jerry opened his door to see Edgar race by, the Dean in hot pursuit. He closed the door again. His phone rang once more. He watched it until it stopped and his answering message began, but there was no message. Nobody at the other end.

"It's not just you, Dad," Margaret said after the waiter had brought them their coffee. Margaret had also ordered a giant cinnamon and apple muffin, and Jerry eyed it jealously. He had vowed to get rid of the additional five pounds he had gathered over the past couple of months, pounds that had led to his ignominious defeat by the Nautilus machine at their last encounter. "It's Mom, too. She's desperately unhappy."

"Defeated in love," Jerry said without sympathy. "It's a tough world."

"Well, you don't have to make it any tougher. Did you and Mom see anybody before you split, a marriage counsellor, someone like that?"

"This is very much none of your business," Jerry said, "but yes, we did go to a marriage counsellor that your mother chose. But the counsellor was so simple-mindedly rapacious, setting up a host of meetings in order to get to 'know us,' as she put it, that neither of us had any faith in her. And of course, the only topic on the agenda was how fast your mother could get out."

"Are you being fair?"

"No. There was the question of whether I would publicly confess my inadequacies as a human being and admit to her nonsensical assertions that I had brutalized her."

"Did you?"

"No, never. I never laid a hand on her. You were there. You saw it all. When would I have done such things?"

"Are you happy now?"

"No, of course not. Only lunatics are happy. The world is not intended to deliver happiness. But I am surviving. I get up in the morning. I do my job. I worry about my health. I walk the dog. Or I sometimes walk the dog. It's not a dog that is a joy to walk."

"Have you thought of a reconciliation?"

"What? Not a chance. Not even if hell freezes over."

"We've been talking with Mom. She's reluctant, too, but she's agreed to talk. We want you to see a counsellor and at least explore the option."

Jerry most emphatically did not want to see a counsellor. He had seen counsellors before and had always found it difficult to concentrate on what they said because he kept thinking of the immense expense of the exercise. He knew all the advice they could offer before they began to speak, and he found himself willing to agree to almost anything in order to end the session.

The waiter came back and refilled Jerry's coffee cup. Margaret was drinking an oversized decaf latte, and she seemed small and vulnerable across the table from him. He remembered how serious she had been as a child, how she had always called him "Daddy" until her thirteenth birthday when she had begun to call him "Father," emphasizing the word as if it were a title she had conferred on him and could remove if necessary.

"Promise me one thing," he said to her. "Promise me you won't marry an old man like your sisters did."

"Pete and Leon are not old men," Margaret said. "They're only four or five years older than Cindy and Lise."

"More like ten or twelve," Jerry said. "I always feel like addressing them as 'sir.' Especially Pete. He looks ready for the charnel house. Nearly bald, and what hair he has is greyer than mine." Which was true. Jerry had kept his black hair against the ravages of age, and it was a simple vanity. He knew it was no more than genetic destiny, but it felt like a moral advantage.

"Pete's a decent guy. He works hard and spends a lot of time outdoors. And Cindy loves him. That's the main thing, isn't it?"

Jerry was not sure that love was the main thing. It was

nice, but it didn't seem to have much to do with anything else. He wondered if he had ever been in love with Thelma. He must have been, since he had married her and had fathered three children on her unresisting body, but he couldn't remember any fierce emotion that resembled love as it was portrayed in books and movies. He loved his daughters, or at least he remembered a fierce protectiveness that he felt for them when they were young.

Did anyone love him? Jerry couldn't remember any evidence in the recent past that even his mother loved him.

"It's only because we love you both that we're asking this," Margaret said, as if Jerry's thought had appeared above his head in a balloon, like a comic strip character's.

"I have to think about this," Jerry said. "I may run away instead, join the circus or become a beach bum or something. I don't think it would work, and I'm not sure I even want it to work. It's been a long time. The scars are nicely healed over. I don't think I want to open them again."

"Please," Margaret said. "Do it for us. If you love us, at least make a try. If it still doesn't work, then we'll understand."

Somebody said "Okay," and Jerry realized that it must have been him since there was no one else at the table.

PETE HAD DECIDED TO BUY AN AIRPLANE and learn to fly. That was what accounted for the frosty silence at the breakfast table. Apparently he needed it because modern ranching was a major business, and if you couldn't match the competition, you were finished. "If you can't stand the heat, get out of the kitchen," was how Pete put it, with a kind of folksy rigour that was perhaps designed to enrage Cindy.

"It's not the airplane," Cindy said. " I know you have to

have equipment, and I don't think Pete would make a bad financial decision. It's just that he intends to fly it himself. And he'll crash it for sure and kill himself. Pete thinks too much. He starts thinking and he forgets where is. That's okay if you are on the back of a horse. The horse will get you home. But it's not okay if you are flying an airplane."

"He has to get a licence first," Jerry said, hoping that he might somehow reassure Cindy. "It's pretty tough, and he may not pass the test."

"Sure, just what I need. A man in despair because he failed to pass his test. Men are stupid about those things. You don't understand."

"I am not entirely without experience in the thinking of men," Jerry answered. "Trust me. In the end, Pete is too intelligent to take risks. If he thinks he might kill himself, he won't fly."

"Yes? Well, he's gone out with Leon for his first lesson. On an airplane with skis. I don't need this."

"If he has any problems flying, then Leon will tell him," Lise said, with less reassuring effect than Jerry had managed. "They're like little kids, and this is a game. Wait till they get home, and we'll see what they say. This may blow over, and on the other hand, he may turn out to be a terrific pilot."

It was clear to Jerry that his gender was not in high popularity around the table, and he excused himself to go to work.

"Oh, by the way," Cindy said. "We took Rover to the vet. He's been moping around and drinking piles of water. Turns out he has diabetes and needs a shot of insulin every morning and evening. We started this morning. We're getting him on a six o'clock schedule. A shot in the morning and one in the evening."

"Who is going to get up at six o'clock in the morning?"

"You get up at seven anyway. It's better to do it at six o'clock; then in the evening, you can give it to him before you go out. We learned how to do it at the vet's. You can give him his shot tonight, and we'll show you how."

"I am not going to order my life around the medical needs of an ancient dog," Jerry said. "That mutt has dug up his last flower bed. I'll drop him off at the vet's on the way to work, and I can pick up his ashes on the way home. You can scatter him in the back lane."

"Don't be ridiculous," Cindy said. "You are not going to kill Rover. It would be like executing a member of the family."

"He is not even my dog," Jerry said. "Our relationship has been one of mutual contempt and loathing from day one. As I remember, he's your dog, Cindy. He'll be going back to Alberta. The weather's good there in the fall."

"Actually, he's Lise's dog," Cindy said. "She'll probably want him."

"He's Margaret's," Lise said. "I gave him to Margaret when I went to university in Vancouver." Margaret was still not out of bed, and the news of her ownership would await her when she descended.

"Meetings," Jerry said, and slipped out the door.

THERE WAS A ONE-SENTENCE MESSAGE on his answering machine when Jerry got to his office. Margaret's voice said, "Rover is not my dog," and then there was a sharp click. That left Jerry with the problem of the injections. He was pretty sure that he was incapable of taking the dog to the vet and actually ordering its murder. If that kind of action were available to him, the dog would long since have gone to greener pastures. And he knew that even with the best of intentions he would not be able to keep up the Spartan regimen required to give it its daily injections. He supposed that he would make a fumbling attempt that would result in the dog's dying in slow agony, growing feebler by the day before his very eyes.

The second message was from Shelley. Could he drop over to the office and sign some forms? The university was closing for the Christmas break in a couple of days, and he had to sign some forms so graduate students could get their money and not spend the holidays as guests of the Salvation Army.

Jerry returned the call immediately, more cheerful about communicating with the department than he had been for weeks. "You're too late," he told Shelley. "My signing privileges have been revoked. I have been overthrown. I have been cast out where there is wailing and gnashing of teeth."

"Since when?"

"Since yesterday's meeting of the graduate committee. I have fallen into deep disfavour with the Commander, and he has engineered my downfall. Anderson gave me the word."

"You haven't heard? There was no meeting yesterday. The meeting was cancelled. Four of the members of the committee, including the Commander, have been charged with sexual harassment. The Dean is in a fury. Your position is safe for the moment. The Commander will be too busy defending himself to worry about you. And then there's the chilly climate complaint that should keep the department busy until June at least."

"Whoa!" Jerry said, suddenly filled with disappointment. "That's not fair. I had received my just desserts. Somebody else should get this job."

"Breaks of the game," Shelley told him. "Besides, you only spend a couple of hours a week at this. It can't be ruining your life."

"No," Jerry said. "I guess not. My life is sufficiently

damaged that this is only a small increment to my misery. Who all was charged, and who did the charging?"

"I'm not supposed to say. It's not public knowledge until the Dean announces it."

"So only support staff are permitted to know? Faculty will be kept in the dark. What if I have one of those monsters as a second reader? How can I prevent them from molesting my students?"

"They're not monsters. The Commander. Baxter. Chamberlain. Anderson."

"Anderson?"

"Yes. He assigned a novel with explicit sexual references and made the complainant read it aloud before the class."

"But not me?"

"Not you. Expect to be heading a lot of committees for the next few months."

"Who is the complainant?"

"That I don't know. I really don't. I don't think any of the complaints are likely to hold up in court, but we may have some tense moments before they get there. Especially with this chilly climate thing."

"What is the chilly climate thing?"

"That's still not open to the public, since charges have not actually been made. But apparently one of the members of the department is considering laying charges against unnamed members of the department who have maligned them and prevented their appointment to senior positions."

"That's easily solved," Jerry said. "Make the complainant chair of the graduate committee. Two birds with one stone. And the proper pronoun is 'her,' not 'them.'"

"You assume the complainant is a woman."

"Can men bring chilly climate complaints?"

"Why not?"

Jerry had never really considered why men might not. And when he remembered Pyncheon and his merry men, the idea was not so far out of the ballpark after all.

JERRY LUNCHED ALONE. There was almost no one at The Club. A few hardy agronomists huddled in a far corner. A young family with children, who would have been even worse brats than they were if there had been an audience, supped in the middle ground. With only Jerry and the agronomists to watch, they were reduced to whining at their mother, who responded in elaborate detail to each of their complaints. Her very English accent added a cheerful, British comedy touch to what might otherwise have been a dreary occasion.

The university was decorated in festive fashion. Wreaths hung on doors, and cards and coloured balls hung in windows. There were even a few reusable Christmas trees standing in odd corners, but the place seemed uninhabited. All the doors along the hallways were closed. It was as if a party had been planned, but then the fear of disease had made all the occupants suddenly abandon the place. Jerry found Shelley in her office having a glass of wine with a couple of graduate students. They had come to wait for Jerry to sign the reports that would free their money.

Jerry signed the reports and remarked that he had never had to sign such reports before.

"No," Shelley said. "Usually the Commander signs them. They're supposed to be signed by the chair of the grad committee, but he also has authority to sign them, and he likes signing things, so I save them for him. It kind of makes his day to come in and show his power by signing a bunch of things." It was an indiscreet statement in front of a couple of graduate students, and Jerry realized that she must have had more than the glass of wine she was drinking. The graduate students, both fiercely bearded young men, showed no signs of picking up their forms and leaving. Jerry wondered if they had designs on Shelley's virtue. They were a lot closer to her age than her boyfriend, Al.

"Well, Merry Christmas," Jerry said, turning to leave. Then he added, "And pass my greetings on to Al."

"Al's gone," Shelley said. "He's flown the coop. He was always a turkey." She burst into an almost hysterical laughter, and the bearded pair laughed with her. Jerry didn't know what to say, so he wished them all a Happy New Year and headed out into the snow.

He entered the college through the back door and could see that one door was open. The light shone out into the hallway, making that office seem warm and inviting against the blank closed doors of the others. As he drew nearer, he realized that it was Willie's office, and he nearly went back and around the building to avoid her. Instead, he peeked into the office and wished her Merry Christmas.

"Merry Christmas," she returned, looking up from the batch of papers she was marking. "We don't see much of you around here these days." That was precisely the line he had intended for his next remark, but he saw now that he was on the defensive.

"Lots of family home for the holidays," he told her. "That and the endless demands of graduate students. How are things with Elena?" He regretted the statement before he had even completed making it. It was so clearly none of his business that he shuddered with embarrassment at his own gaucherie.

"Elena," Willie said, "is as much of a pest as usual. But she is working as my research assistant. I posted the position and there was one applicant, Elena, and so I hired her. Actually, she is a terrific research assistant. She spends hours in the library and has found some amazing stuff. And yes, she still writes poetry, though that is not a capital offence. How's your marking going?"

Jerry realized that he had done no marking at all. His papers were stacked neatly on his desk, as pristine as the day they were written. He thought of all the analyses of patriarchy and image patterns, the struggle between good and evil as expressed through images of darkness and light that he was going to have to read, and a wave of disgust swept over him that was fully physical.

"Are you all right?" Willie asked, getting up from her desk. "You look as if you had seen a ghost."

"I'm fine," Jerry said. "It was a passing thing. Whenever I think of marking, I feel faint. One of these days I'm going to give a machine-marked test in Canadian poetry. All the questions will be either true or false, and I will feed the answers into a computer and await the results."

"You mean the answers," Willie said. "It is the answers that are true or false, not the questions."

"Whichever," Jerry replied, unwilling to commit himself on the point of grammar until he had figured it out. "Anyway, things are going all right for you?"

"Alone in my monastic cell," she said. "Other people have lives, I have student essays. And my book. The final, definitive study of something or other that will make me so famous that I will be hired away by Harvard or Yale and go on to fame and riches and the deep respect of my peers."

"Ah, yes," Jerry said. "The very book that I myself am writing. It will be a race for publication and may the best man win."

"Or woman."

"Yes, them too. Would you like to get some coffee?"

Willie had returned to her desk and was fiddling with her pen. "No. Or yes, I'd like some coffee, but I am going to resist any form of gratification until these are finished. I've only got ten left, and I'm not leaving until they are done."

"Well," Jerry said. "Have fun." And he made his way to his office, unsure what he had learned. She had intimated that she was only in a professional relationship with Elena, but she hadn't actually said so, and he hadn't asked her. And it really wasn't any of his business.

Jerry arrived at the Java Shoppe about five minutes late, because a young woman and an older man got into a fender bender in front of him. In their efforts to avoid a collision, each had swerved so that they came to rest completely blocking traffic. There seemed to be very little damage, but the pair went through an elaborate procedure of exchanging addresses and showing each other cards that took about fifteen minutes. The young woman in particular had difficulty finding her information, and searched for what seemed ages in a purse so large she could have lived out of it. He would have turned around, but the drivers beside him and behind him had pulled up very close, and seemed in no hurry themselves. The result was that when Jerry walked through the doors of the Java Shoppe, he was in a silent rage.

Debbie was not there. The Java Shoppe was on the outskirts of the university and Jerry had expected it to be empty. Instead, it was filled with professors, as if they did not really want to go to the university, but still wanted to get as close as they could without actually entering the premises. Jerry recognized several of the union leaders in fierce debate at a far table, and thought nostalgically of the strike. Perhaps they were planning another. It couldn't happen soon enough.

All but one of the tables was full. A lone woman sipped

her coffee at the table nearest the window, and, as Jerry approached, he recognized Julia Helmsholm, despite the fact that she was fully clothed. He glanced at the title of the book she was reading: *Great Expectations.*

"Dickens," he said, taking the seat across from her.

"Kathy Acker," she said.

"My memory must be failing me. I was sure that Dickens had written *Great Expectations.*"

"He did. But so did Kathy Acker. I prefer her version."

Jerry had seen Kathy Acker's name before, and it came to him now. Anderson had supervised an MA thesis on Kathy Acker.

"Why do you prefer her version?" he asked.

"Better pornography," she said. "More convincing."

"I hadn't realized that Dickens was even in the running. I hadn't actually thought of his work as pornography."

"Better reread it," Julia said.

"Has Anderson been leading you astray, taking you from the simple life of the stripper into the evils of English literature?"

"No, actually, it was me who introduced him to Kathy Acker's work. He was woefully uninformed about good pornography. You guys in the English Department don't get out much. Too much Trollope and Meredith can rot the brain."

Jerry remembered her training. She had taken more courses in logic than he was willing to confront over coffee, and so he changed the topic.

"How's Anderson?" he asked. "How's the cottage in France?"

"Anderson's fine. He's taking care of the kids. This is Mother's Morning Out. And the cottage in France is nearly paid for. One more year, and we're out of here."

"Does Anderson know this?"

"Yes. He doesn't really want to teach Critical Theory. He

actually wants to write a novel. And if he doesn't do it soon, he never will."

Anderson had never confessed this fantasy to Jerry, and now, put so plainly in the open air of the coffee shop, it seemed mildly obscene, like a desire to cross-dress that might be understandable but should be kept secret.

"Anderson a novelist?"

"Why not?"

"Well, don't you have to serve an apprenticeship? Start with occasional poems in literary journals, then a chapbook, a well-reviewed collection of linked short stories, a couple of radio interviews, an appearance on television and finally the major work, applause, fame, fortune."

"Anderson has published quite a lot of stories, but he writes under a pseudonym."

"Let me guess. He's actually John Updike?"

"Don't be cruel. What about you? What are you doing with your own life?"

"I don't do anything with my life. Life is a thing that happens to me. I have given up any hope of ever being in control of it. It's a roller-coaster ride to the grave, and I'm picking up momentum on the way down."

"That's pretty defeatist. Don't you have any fantasy of escape?"

"Australia," Jerry told her. "I've got an old college roommate who lives in Tasmania. He made a fortune in the aluminum siding business, and he wants me to come to Australia. Says he'll give me a job."

"Selling aluminum siding door-to-door?"

"No. He has lots of businesses. He owns a string of bookstores, and he's looking for a manager."

"Do you think you could manage a bookstore?"

"Sure, it isn't rocket science. You buy books and you sell them. Have you seen some of those guys who run bookstores?"

Just then, Debbie arrived. She was in a navy-blue power suit and she carried a briefcase. She looked both competent and beautiful, like one of those models they hire for television ads about banks. Jerry introduced her to Julia.

"Jerry here has been telling me his plans to run off to Australia," Julia said, getting up and putting on her coat.

"Tasmania, actually," Jerry said. "Van Diemen's land. That's where criminals go."

"I thought Tasmania was in Africa."

"That's Tanganyika. But it would also do in a pinch."

"Actually, I knew that. My mother lives in Wellington. I've actually been to Tasmania."

"Have fun," Julia told them. "I'm off to release the big guy from the kids so he can go and do whatever it is he does. We run our affairs as a sort of tag-team wrestling match." They watched her as she made her way out of the coffee shop.

"I've seen her somewhere before," Debbie said. "Does she work at the college?"

"You probably didn't recognize her with clothes. Remember the bar the other night? The stripper?"

"You've taken to meeting strippers for coffee?"

"Actually, she's almost a member of the department. Nietzsche is her specialty. That and artificial intelligence."

"Artificial intelligence?"

"The kind of intelligence in which we specialize. As opposed to real intelligence."

"You disappeared suddenly. I walked into the washroom for a minute and when I came back you had vanished."

"An important meeting of arsonists. We were meeting to burn down a barn, and I couldn't take a chance on being late and missing the fun."

"You burned down a barn?"

"It was just a little barn. It didn't even have any animals in it."

"Even so."

"I know. It's an awful habit and I'm trying to quit. You're still keeping bad company I see."

"Who, Jocko?"

"And Al Green. Both are famous debauchers of youth and breakers of hearts."

"Are you jealous?"

Jerry considered. She was right. He was jealous. "Yes," he answered. "I don't know why but that's probably correct. I'd prefer to think of this as friendly counsel, but then I'm famous for my powers of self-deception. Just be aware that any enterprise you enter with them is probably doomed to some new enthusiasms on their part."

"So I'll be used, then flung aside like a dirty shirt?"

"That's not the metaphor I would have chosen, but it will do."

"If you are concerned about my virtue, don't worry. I am without virtue, as you already know. I can handle myself without your help."

"I'm sorry. Of course you can."

"Do you have any other avuncular advice?"

"You've changed the way you dress. You've changed the way you speak. Is this all part of some vast changeover?"

"You don't like it? You prefer the waif?"

"No. But it's such a sweeping change. Was the Debbie I met a few weeks ago an act that you staged?"

"No. Or yes. We're all acting. You're pretending to be a professor. Jocko's pretending to be an artist. Al is pretending to be a media star. Julia, or whatever her name is, is pretending to be a stripper. I've decided to broaden my role, to add a few missing details to the script."

"Why don't you run away with me to Tasmania? We could live in a grass hut and grow old together. Or you could grow old. I'm already there, so there's not much for me to do."

"Sure, when do you want to go?"

"Another fantasy ruined. You were supposed to say that it was impossible."

"You only fantasize about the impossible?"

"Pretty much. Actually, you called this meeting. You had something you wanted to ask me about."

"That's right," Debbie said. "Are you ready?"

"Fire away."

"I'm looking for investors for a project that could make a lot of money," Debbie said.

"Well, count me out right from the start. I'm into short-term investments in bread and milk. I use the dipstick method of accounting. I go to the bank and ask them if I have any money. If they say yes, then I take it and spend it. Lately there haven't been many yesses."

"I wasn't thinking about you. I was looking for some advice. I'm new to the city. I don't really know who has money and who hasn't."

"Doctors. Doctors have all the money. And dentists, or especially dentists. They have even more money than doctors have. You just go to, for instance, a dentist, and when you're in the chair and the dentist tells you to say 'ah,' and peers into your mouth, you ask him for money. It's the element of surprise. Gets them every time."

"No, be serious."

"Okay. Why do you need this money?"

"Okay," Debbie said, and she drew a deep breath and pushed back a stray lock of hair that had fallen over her left eye. Her hair was a rich, dark brown, and a shaft of sunlight through the window suddenly brightened it to a deep auburn that verged on red. The effect was so startling that Jerry would have found it contrived in a movie. She seemed suddenly so beautiful that he was filled with despair. He seemed doomed to a life of unwanted celibacy or the option of a return to Thelma or the even more horrible option of Evelyn, though even there he had been rejected. He reminded himself that he had actually slept with the woman before him, but that seemed less real than any of his fantasies. He opened his mouth to ask her to marry him and realized that she had gone on speaking, and he had missed at least the first part of her statement.

What he heard was, "amazing script, and so they've asked me to help organize the financial backing. They're also hoping for Telefilm and a number of other agencies, but I'm mostly concerned with private funding. Doctors and dentists, like you said. And lawyers. And retired people who have a bit of money to play with."

"Whom are we talking about?" Jerry asked. He had the horrible fear that she had said Jocko Degraves and Al Green, and he was certain that if they had written the script for a movie, then it was going to be a disaster.

"You weren't listening," Debbie said. "You were looking out the window and not paying any attention to what I was saying." She had brought out an envelope with some papers from her purse and now she put it back and was making preparations to get up and leave.

"I was not looking out the window. I was looking at you. You can't go around looking like that and expect people to be able to concentrate on what you are saying."

"What are you talking about?"

"You. You can't be so beautiful that people forget about everything else and just look at you. It isn't fair. And how are you going to get all those doctors and dentists to pay attention to your pitch if all they want to do is go to bed with you?"

"There are women doctors and dentists too, you know."

"Yes I do know. Them too. It is no longer politically correct to discriminate between genders in the matter of lust. They too will yearn for you and forget what you are saying."

"You seemed to be able to resist me quite nicely."

"I did not. You came as an innocent guest to my house and I lay in wait and debauched you when your guard was down."

"You did not. If anybody did the debauching, it was me."

"Let's try it again and determine once and for all who is at fault."

"No, Jerry, that isn't going to work. I've got a job and an apartment and I'm trying to make a life for myself. You've got to work out what you are going to do with the rest of your life. Right now, anything we tried would only be a general disaster."

"But maybe later? Maybe next week?"

"Not next week. Not next month. Maybe sometime. Now are you going to listen to me?"

"Shoot." Jerry said. "Let me have it with both barrels."

Debbie outlined the plan. The film was going to be directed by David Webb. Webb had made a series of experimental films that had made him internationally famous. He had won dozens of awards. Now he was going to make a straight-ahead realist story about a mysterious disease that strikes a small Saskatchewan town. There'd also be a love story. The script was incredible. It was going to be an enormous hit. It could easily be sold to Hollywood, but they wanted to keep it local. Neither Al Green nor Jocko Degraves had anything to do with it, other than they were both blown away by the idea, and they had each invested five thousand dollars in it.

"Where do those guys get five thousand dollars?" Jerry asked. "Why would they invest in something as risky as a film?"

"Because I asked them to. That was why I was having lunch with them at The Club."

"And at the Pub?"

"Jerry, they're just friends. We play on the same hockey team."

"What? You're a hockey player?"

"It's a fun league. Like slow-pitch baseball. We play on an outdoor rink with a soft rubber ball instead of a puck, and then we go for a few beers."

"Let me take you away from all this," Jerry said. "Hockey's a rough game. You'll be injured, you'll get a gimpy knee, like Bobby Orr, and have to sit around in armchairs for the rest of your life. You've seen him on TV, dressed in shorts and watching the surf roll in on some Caribbean island. You don't want that to happen to you."

"No, Jerry. Tell me about investors."

"Okay," Jerry said. "I'll introduce you to my cousin Steven. He owns the biggest hog operation in the Interlake area. He's rolling in money. If he likes you, he'll invest."

"Hogs?" Debbie said.

"Money is money," Jerry told her. "If you can't stand a little pigshit, keep out of the kitchen."

"That's a mixed metaphor."

"Yes, I know. I mix them myself."

"And Steven really has money?"

"Steven has his own airplanes. Note the plural. He owns a fishing resort which he bought and closed so that he can use it himself for two weeks a year. He owns condos in Arizona and in Barbados. He owns snowmobiles and sailboats and racing cars and horses and antique French furniture. He even hires someone to come over and pat his dog."

"Perhaps I should marry him instead?"

"Not a chance. He's got a daughter he calls Princess, who is the most spoiled sixteen-year-old in the world. He spends half his time thinking up things to buy her. If he fools around, his wife will take her away, and he'll never see her again. He takes no chances."

"But they're not happy, those people. Money can't buy happiness."

"They're giving it their best shot. And in the meantime, they're happier than anyone else I know. Disaster could strike them right now, and they'd still have used up more than their fair allotment of happiness for one lifetime. That's a myth, you know, that story that rich people are unhappy. It's spread by rich people who don't want the proletariat to revolt. Actually, they're much happier than us."

The waitress came by and took away their cups without asking whether they wanted a refill. Jerry took that to be a less than gentle hint that it was time to leave. Debbie looked at her watch and sighed.

"I've got to get back to work," she said.

"You like your work?" Jerry asked.

"No, I hate it. It's not the particular work that I hate. I hate work in general. You know, I had decided that I wanted to settle down, to take charge of my life, to make something of myself. Now I'm not so sure."

"The old biological clock?"

"No. That clock can run itself down for all of me. Kids sound like an awful lot of work."

"They are," Jerry affirmed. "And there's a fifty-fifty chance that some of them could turn out to be daughters. It's just not worth taking the chance."

"I was a daughter, once."

"And I'm sure you were responsible for many a grey hair. And speaking of daughters, I've got to go buy some presents. It's only a couple of days to Christmas, and I haven't even begun my shopping."

The thought of shopping filled Jerry with guilt, as it always had done. And with the guilt came another memory. A note from Margaret that she had slipped into his pocket as he had left that morning. He hadn't looked at it then and had put the matter out of his mind until now. He reached into his pocket, unfolded the note and read it. It said only, "Dad, we've set up an appointment for you and Mum at four this afternoon." There was also a card that read Dr. Leonard Workman, Family Counsellor. Jerry groaned.

"Something wrong?" Something was very wrong indeed. He was going to meet with a counsellor who would try to convince him that he should reconcile with Thelma. There was hardly anyone alive he would less like to reconcile with than Thelma, and he was pretty sure that even if he did, the relationship couldn't last a week.

"No," Jerry told her. "I've got to pick up something on the way home."

THE WAY HOME WAS CIRCUITOUS. Jerry drove in heavy pre-Christmas traffic to the only store in which he had ever shopped for women's Christmas presents. It was called Milly's, and it was where Thelma and all of his daughters had shopped in the old days. It was on a street that he remembered as being in one of those new areas full of little fancy boutiques. It was no longer a fashionable place. Many of the store windows were boarded over, there was plenty of parking on the street and no sign of foot traffic. Milly's, however, was open, and, to his untrained eye, the merchandise seemed as elegant as ever. It was certainly as expensive. He found a pile of sweaters, originally three hundred dollars each, reduced to one hundred and fifty. The clerk hovered a few feet from him like a female lion unsure whether the prey she was stalking was too large to take down without calling for help.

"I'll take three of those," Jerry said.

"Three?" the clerk asked with a rising inflection that hinted at disbelief.

"Four," Jerry said. "Make it four." If Thelma was going to be there for Christmas, he could avoid any stress by simply including her in the round of presents as if nothing had happened, as if it were still the old days when the girls were young and Thelma, though she probably didn't love him even then, had at least been willing to play out the rules of the marriage game.

"Which colours would you like?" The clerk still seemed doubtful that such a bulk order was actually going to be consummated. She was a tall woman, so thin she seemed ethereal, likely to be blown away by the slightest breeze. She smelled faintly of powder and something that reminded him of cinnamon.

"One of each," he said, choosing them from the pile.

"And what sizes would you like?"

"Doesn't matter," Jerry told her. "They'll all be back here Boxing Day exchanging them for something else."

THE COUNSELLOR'S OFFICE was in a small mall in a suburb named Woodridge, though the almost total absence of trees suggested that it was an optimistic prediction of the future rather than an accurate description of landscape. Low, flat, middle-class housing stretched for miles in every direction, and at each corner, small self-important children in blaze-red vests waved flags and reduced traffic to a crawl, though only a few stray children actually seemed to be on the way home. Everywhere there were signs of the new: new houses, new cars, new malls, new traffic signs. The existence of a marriage counsellor in the midst of such apparent optimism suggested a darker side to the picture of North American progress.

Or perhaps the customers were all older, more cynical folk

from settled parts of the city, and the location was intended to remind them of their earlier years of soccer and ballet lessons and meetings with teachers. The memory of those days struck Jerry with a shiver that he identified as despair. He would not go back to them even to regain a youthful body and a sense of purpose.

Jerry was early despite the best efforts of the school patrols to delay him. The counsellor's office was on the second floor of the central building, the only two-storey space in the mall. Jerry walked up the central staircase rather than taking the elevator, which struck him as a sign of decadence. If people insisted on riding elevators in two-storey buildings, the people of the North would swoop down and destroy the fragile civilization he inhabited.

He stopped at the door, hesitated a second, then turned and fled down the steps. He wasn't certain whether he was abandoning the interview or was merely going to look around the mall rather than sit in a waiting room. He had originally imagined a waiting room something like a doctor's or dentist's, where a receptionist made entries in a book and people sat around reading out-of-date magazines, but he had gone this route once before, when Thelma was preparing him for her leaving. There would be no receptionist, no other people, only a couple of hard chairs and some pamphlets from a social-work organization.

He found himself in a store that imported things from third-world countries. At the entrance was a thermos full of coffee that had been bought from third-world ethical coffee producers, and could be purchased at two dollars a cup. You could order beans for a mere twelve dollars a pound in a minimum order of six pounds. Jerry tried the coffee. It was okay, neither better nor worse than other coffee he drank. The ethics of the producers had apparently nothing to do with the taste of their product.

The sheer profusion of carved giraffes, alabaster eggs, wicker baskets and whirligigs of various kinds overwhelmed him, and he moved on to a health-food store next door. The smells there were meant to be medicinal, but they reminded Jerry of nausea. The other stores were mall regulars, shoe stores and athletic stores and women's clothing places. The fluorescent lights made everything seem slightly green to Jerry, but he thought that must be his imagination. The designers of malls would have discovered something so obvious and introduced some other colour designed to make you buy. It must be his own fault, a reflection of his own inner spirit that altered the quality of light.

And it was that awareness of his own take on the world that made Jerry decide to go back to the counsellor's office. Perhaps his daughters were right. Perhaps the world took on the shape he had wished it to have, took its lead from his own inner spirit. And if he were colouring his world a bilious green, then only he could change it. It was time to buck up, to face reality, to take his medicine like a man. Some cynical part of his psyche suggested that he hadn't the chance of a snowball in hell of changing anything, but he denied it, put it into the back of his consciousness, left it to stew in its own juices.

Thelma was sitting in a chair, waiting, when Jerry arrived. He glanced at his watch and noticed that he was five minutes late. The clock on the wall disagreed. It said he was right on time, and Jerry wondered why the counsellor kept the clock slow. He could hardly have failed to notice, and Jerry imagined that it might be a face-saving technique for someone who was always five minutes late. Someone like Thelma.

"Right on time," Jerry said, mustering up cheerfulness as a defense.

"I thought I was going to be late," Thelma said. "I hate being late."

"It's snowing," Jerry said.

"Yes."

"They say there's a system moving in. They say we could have a nasty storm in the next couple of days."

"They always say things like that. And they're always wrong."

Just then the counsellor appeared. Jerry had been expecting a cheerful, balding man who made puns and talked like a high-school guidance counsellor. He was not expecting the thin, tall, dishevelled woman who looked as if she had rushed in from a meeting with her lover. Her lipstick was either smeared or else carelessly applied. She had high cheekbones and what Jerry thought of as a mobile mouth. She seemed to chew her words before speaking them.

"Come in," she said, leading them down the hallway to an office that was starkly modern, except that the desk in the corner was messy. The chairs were leather and stainless steel but surprisingly comfortable. Jerry and Thelma sat across from each other, over a low glass table with a sculpture of a black, winged horse and a couple of unlit candles. Her name was Karla Manfred, she said. Leonard Workman was out of town, and she was filling in for him. Did they mind?

Jerry was glad there had been a substitution. The very name Workman did not bode well. Thelma simply nodded.

"You're not here to save your marriage," she said. "You're here because whatever wrecked it in the first place is no worse than what you've got now. You want to figure out what to do next."

"Don't you want us to explain what happened?" Thelma asked.

"We've got one hour," Karla said. "You both know you aren't coming back to see me again. You are probably both wondering what you're doing here in the first place. So there's no time to figure out what went wrong or to assign blame. If you don't want to waste a couple of hundred dollars, let's abandon the shit and see if there's any strategy that has the remotest chance of success."

It was more expensive than Jerry expected, and he knew he was going to be the one to pay for it.

"We can't talk about anything," Thelma said. "Jerry does not talk about things. He ambushes every conversation with puns and jokes and exotic literary quotations."

"True," Jerry added. "It's a strategy that has kept me alive for fifty years. Not happy, but alive."

"Is it something you can change?" the counsellor asked. She was playing with her pencil, twisting it around a lock of her hair, and Jerry thought that this must be bad counsellor procedure, distracting your subjects from the chore at hand.

"No," Jerry said, with what he thought was honesty.

"No," Thelma echoed.

"Good," the counsellor said. "That's one thing out of the way. Jerry is not going to change. And you, what's the thing about you that you think needs changing, or Jerry thinks you need to change?"

"Falling in love with other people," Thelma said.

"Or more precisely, other women," Jerry added.

"Would it be better if it were men?" Karla asked.

"No, I guess not." Jerry wasn't sure if that was right. It struck him now that it might have been worse if she had fallen in love with another man. Her present relationship might be explained as biology or as a new social phenomenon. If it had been another man, Jerry would merely have been cuckolded, and he would enter the history of sad cuckolds. "Actually," he said, "a man would probably have been as difficult." He paused. "More difficult, actually."

"And you?" Karla turned to Thelma. "What do you have to say?"

"I'm not in love with anybody at the moment. And not likely to be in the near future."

"Well, that's another problem out of the way. Why are you here?"

"Our daughters set this up," Thelma said. "I guess it was their idea." Jerry nodded agreement.

"But you came. Each of you got into your car and drove here. You walked all the way up the staircase and sat in the waiting room together. And now you are sitting here talking to me. You could have left at any moment. You could have chosen not to come. Either or both of you could still leave right now." She looked toward the door, as if it might suddenly swing open. Nobody spoke for a full minute.

"So you're still here. Now we just have to figure out what you want."

That was precisely the problem and always had been the problem. What did he want? He certainly didn't want to recapture his youth or to go back to the early days of his marriage. He had been in love with Thelma, he was pretty sure of that. He remembered desire, and he remembered quiet barbecues and the gentle excitement of planning trips. There had been time then for everything. Now, he never had time for anything. Where had the time gone?

He looked at Thelma, and then turned away. He didn't want to appear to be sizing her up as if he were planning to buy a used car, though he supposed that was something allied to what he was doing. Kicking her tires.

Thelma was still in remarkably good shape for her age. Her hair was streaked with grey, but it still held its colour. She had obviously been exercising, because she was toned and fit. She had dressed up for the interview, and Jerry felt a stir of sympathy. Why did you want to look nice for someone you had never met and who was professionally committed to not judging you? Or maybe she had dressed up for him. She was wearing a dress suit with a long skirt, like a lawyer who intended to go out to dinner after a day in court, and she did look professional.

"I want some stability," she told the counsellor. "I want to settle into old age with a sense of where I might be in the next twenty years. I want the whole world to slow down. I want to make quilts, and I want to garden and I want to write a novel."

Jerry was startled. This was the first he had heard of Thelma's literary ambitions, and he was about to tease her about her historic distaste for literature, but he thought better of it. He was here. Whatever happened, he was not going to destroy the process in advance.

"And you?" the counsellor asked. "What do you want?"

Her question was so ludicrously serious that Jerry nearly opted for peace in the Middle East. The counsellor had by now so twisted the pencil in her hair that it had worked its way into a bun. It made her resemble a woman from one of those African tribes that had been so popular in the *National Geographic*s of his youth, except that she was fully clothed from the waist up. It was this kind of mental rambling that kept getting him into trouble, Jerry thought, and he forced his mind back to the subject at hand. What did he want?

He wanted the sex life of a pasha. He wanted wealth beyond counting. He wanted the counsellor herself, naked to the waist. He wanted to concentrate on what the counsellor had said. He wanted to run away.

"Me?" he asked. "What do I want?"

"Yes," she said. "You."

Jerry tried to concentrate. He didn't want Evelyn, and luckily, she didn't want him. He wanted Willie, but at that precise moment he couldn't remember what she looked like. He wanted Debbie very badly but, for some reason he couldn't articulate, that seemed out of the question. He didn't want his job. Visions of Australia danced in his head, kangaroos and wallabies and kookaburras in fig trees.

"Herbs," Jerry said. "I want to grow seventy-seven different types of herbs. I want to learn to tango. I want to play the piano."

The lamp behind the counsellor was designed to look like a giant stainless steel and plastic tulip. The lamp had begun to twirl behind her in a slow dance. Jerry did not want to grow herbs. He did not want to tango or to play the piano.

"I want time," Jerry said. "I want moments of peace."

Thelma was enthusiastic. "That is precisely what I want. Get out of the rat race. Move to Galiano or someplace like that, an island, and live a life that just slows down. We could do that." She looked at Jerry, and he thought he saw real affection in her eyes. The sun was shining through the window with far more brilliance than was appropriate for the season.

"Are you both willing to try? To get together and see if you can make it work?" the counsellor asked. "What have you got to lose? You can only fail, and if you do, you'll be no worse than you are right now." Jerry had not noticed the music in the background but it was much louder now, and it nearly drowned out the counsellor's words. The sun was even brighter, and the tulips were dancing a dance of joy.

"Yes," Thelma said. "Yes, I'd be willing to try."

"Yes. Oh God, yes." Jerry heard a voice that he identified as his own. The tulips had begun to glow. Time stretched infinitely before him, and Jerry slipped gratefully from his chair onto the floor where he stretched out luxuriously and slept.

JERRY WAS SUFFOCATING. He had been buried deep in snow. An avalanche he had not been expecting had hit him from somewhere, and he was frantically trying to fight his way out. Then, finally, he saw light and struggled out into the dawn. He untangled himself from the feather quilt that had seized him and sat up in his own bed. He had a terrible hangover, and he vowed to himself that he would give up alcohol forever. Then he remembered that he had not had anything to drink. In the thin early light he tried to make sense of what had happened. He had slid onto the floor, he remembered that. He had spoken with a marriage counsellor, an African woman with a bone in her hair. It had been in a jungle with enormous tulips and they had danced a tango.

Someone stirred on the other side of the bed, and Jerry realized with horror that he was not alone. A figure with dark hair streaked with grey was curled up in a blanket. Thelma.

Jerry leaped from the bed as if he had been bitten by a snake. He dressed as quietly as could and crept down the stairs. He could hear male snoring in the living room, and he tiptoed to the door and let himself out. His car was parked on the street, but he left it there and walked to the bus stop. He got on the first bus that came by, and it took him all the way to the university. As they travelled down the snow-covered street he tried to recreate the events of yesterday. He had been so terribly tired. They had wanted him to go to a doctor, but he had refused. He had driven home. He knew that because he had parked in a mall and forgotten where his car was and he had looked for a long time before he found it.

Why had he been at the mall? Then he remembered that he had seen a doctor after all. He had gone to a walk-in clinic and waited a long time in the waiting room. He had read an old copy of *National Geographic*. Could that be true? Stress, the doctor had told him. He had to take some time off. In the meantime he was to take half an Aspirin a day and make an appointment to see his own doctor. But he didn't have a doctor. When he had split up with Thelma, she had got the doctor, and he hadn't got himself a new one. He would have to find a doctor.

Then memory came in a flood. He had not been alone. Thelma had come with him. She had waited in the waiting room. They had driven home together. They had bought a pizza on the way, and a bottle of red wine. Then he had started to drink Scotch. Pete had a bottle of Glenfiddich, and Jerry had drunk most of it. He remembered calling Pete an asshole and Leon an incompetent loser before he had stumbled up to bed.

He felt much better now. He had a hangover. He knew how to deal with that. At least he had not suffered a stroke. Nothing irreparable had happened to his brain. He could apologize to Pete and Leon. His daughters had spent the evening in the kitchen with Thelma. They had seemed to accept Jerry's drunkenness as his due, and had helped him up the stairs and into bed.

And yet, there was Thelma in his bed. Something would have to be done about that. In the cold light of the morning he was sure that he had suffered an enormous tactical loss, that he had made some military blunder on a cosmic scale that was going to be almost impossible to redress. But he was alive, and, though he had only stragglers for troops, he could carry on. It would have to be guerilla war from now on, but there was still hope.

The bus pulled up at the stop in front of the library, and he got off. There was no other sign of life on the campus, nobody walking on the sidewalks, no cars either driving or parked, no lights in any of the windows. He crossed the quadrangle and walked between the Pharmacy Building and the Art School and down the path to the college.

The back door was locked, and Jerry realized that he had not signed out a key for the holiday period. He had an ancient key that had been given to him when he had first come to teach at the university, but he was sure they must have changed the locks by now.

The key worked, and Jerry was grateful for the inefficiency of the college that permitted ancient locks to continue to function with ordinary keys when the rest of the university had converted to electronic locks that opened with identity cards. Or had they actually converted? There had been talk about changing them, but Jerry didn't remember ever having seen such an electronic key. At any rate, the key worked, as did the key to his office.

The telephone on his desk flashed its red light, but Jerry ignored it. He spread his coat on the floor, took off his sweater and bunched it into a pillow, then stretched out and slept a deep, dreamless sleep.

JERRY AWOKE TO A DEEP MALE VOICE telling him it was hot.

"Sunshine every day. Beaches with surf. The best wine in the world. Paradise, in short," the voice said. "And you're missing it. Tell you a secret. Hell isn't hot. It's cold. Thirty below. Think about that, Buddy, and buy that ticket."

Jerry did think about it. He looked out his window at the smoke that didn't rise from chimneys but crept over the edges and slid down roofs. He surveyed the snow that was falling gently in large flakes and the icicle that had begun to grow from the air-conditioner in his window but had interrupted its growth until warmer weather, when a thaw would add to its length. He was living in a place where icicles were a sign that it was warming up.

His office was a mess. There was no denying that. Mail

had accumulated on his desk as if it bred there and multiplied. He regarded himself as ruthless in his treatment of mail when compared to his fellows. Anderson was apparently incapable of throwing out even a publisher's catalogue, and piles of ancient mail grew like stalactites towards the ceiling. Evelyn, for all her fastidiousness, was a relentless collector of desk copies, and her shelves were overloaded with outdated anthologies. By comparison, he was meticulous.

Nevertheless, his office was a mess, and, if he was going to be starting a new life, as he supposed he must be, given what had happened over the last day or so, then he had better start with a clean slate.

Apparently the mail had not actually multiplied on his desk. He was the victim of a university-wide strategy. People who were looking for breathing space waited until the last possible second, then posted mail that required immediate action but was guaranteed a two-week reprieve, since the recipients would not get it until they returned after the new year. It was a device that Jerry had used himself on more than one occasion. Usually, it would have mouldered in his mailbox until he got back, but then Mary Jane, the helpful college secretary, must have decided as a last act to leave her work complete, the mailboxes uncluttered. Perhaps she too had fantasies about Australia.

Jerry was tempted by the red light on his telephone, but he resisted. It would have to wait its turn until he had completed his clean-up. He started with books that were nested in small clumps around the room and returned them to their place in alphabetic order on his shelves. Partway through the operation he began to feel a familiar sense of despair as he realized that he was never going to reread most of the books he had treasured and that he had no intention of reading most of the books he had not yet opened.

In a moment of inspiration, he began to carry them out

his office door and pile them in the hallway. When he was finished, he had an enormous pile that stretched along the hallway right to the door of the next office. There were about forty books left in his office. He took a piece of paper, wrote the words FREE BOOKS on it, and taped it to the pile in the hallway.

McPherson had apparently bought a new computer, and the box lay invitingly in the hallway. Jerry seized it and began to sort files out of his filing cabinet. After a few minutes, the same feeling of panic and ennui that had affected him with the books struck him again. He took the file that was labelled "Graduate Studies" and put it on the desk with his mail. Then he emptied all the files from the filing cabinet into the computer box and dragged it into the hallway. The room was beginning to look neat.

The desk was next. Nothing there was salvageable. He brought back the computer box and emptied all the drawers into it. In a moment, he realized what it must be like to drown. His life flashed before him in random order: pictures of the girls as children, old floppy disks that wouldn't work in any computer that still functioned, a horde of ancient pay slips, envelopes whose edges were browned with age, letterhead that reduced his rank to assistant professor, thousands of paper clips, pens that had been dried up and out of ink for decades, stamps he had ripped from letters from Mozambique and Surinam on the chance that he might one day become a collector, copper coins, thumb tacks, screws, an old razor, bottles of pills, lozenges, a roll of Tums, a Christmas decoration made from *papier mâché*, one leather glove, pages ripped from a magazine, a mask made from a false nose and glasses.

He saved only the mask and dumped the rest into the computer box. The mask was the only thing he couldn't remember ever having seen before, and so it seemed to gain a higher ontological status. It was the sole mystery in a grab bag of dreary memories. He dragged the box, heavier now, into the hallway, and wrote "Garbage" on it.

He felt much better now. He felt like a man who was doing a favour to a cousin's widow, cleaning up the effects after the funeral so that she would not have to go through the agony of fearing that she might discover something she didn't want to know. He felt that he had only a distant relationship with the owner of these things he was dispensing with. He went down the hall to the small kitchen and found a grimy dishcloth, which he wrung out and took back to his office. After he had wiped down all the shelves and the filing cabinet, the room gleamed with optimism. It was a place where things could be done, decisions could be made.

The first piece of mail was a notice that his article on nineteenth-century Canadian magazines in Upper Canada had been accepted for publication. The editor apologized for the delay, but Jerry's article had been inadvertently misfiled, and had only recently come to light. It would appear in the summer issue.

Jerry calculated. It had been inadvertently lost for nineteen years. And yet, he was certain that it would be as timely as any other article in the issue. That was the beauty of academic life. It had a timelessness that made any other kind of life seem futile and rushed. He couldn't remember what the article was about, could not for the life of him remember the name of a single nineteenth-century magazine. Or wait. *The Canadian Punch.* Then they came back to him in a rush. *Grip. The Canadian Monthly. Rose-Belford's Monthly. The Anglo-American Review. The British American Review. The Literary Garland.* The room seemed to fill with choking dust as he thought of the archives he had sat in, the awful microfilm he had read.

The next letter was a note from the Dean. It asked that he

provide a two- or three-page report on the graduate program in English, along with recommendations on ways in which it could be made more efficient. Could he please send it to the Dean via his department head by at the latest the twentieth of December? Jerry threw it into the wastebasket.

The next was a handwritten note from Orest and Norma Jean. It was written in Madrid. They were sitting in the Prado looking at Hieronymous Bosch's *Garden of Delights*. Orest had decided to play basketball in Italy, and Norma Jean had decided to accompany him. She had given up on her thesis again. They wanted to thank Jerry for bringing them together and had already decided to name their first-born after him.

The letter was written in an elegant, flowing, feminine script, and at its bottom were a few words in a large, clumsy male script expressing the same sentiments in a terser prose. Jerry hoped that the feminine script would prove to be Orest's and the brutal kidnapper's script would be Norma Jean's, but that was too much to hope for. Cliché triumphed.

The other letters were easy. Most of them demanded that he sign and return before the twentieth or dire things would happen. Scholarships would go unclaimed, people would be prevented from entering programs, graduate students would not get their cheques before Christmas. All this was to be his fault for inefficiency. Jerry knew that none of the dire things would happen. Everybody had set up a paper trail to pass on responsibility if something should go wrong, but the great amorphous mess of the university would mean that nobody would actually have to take responsibility for anything.

That left only the telephone. Jerry looked at it for a long time. He was tempted to erase all messages without listening to them, but he had begun to feel that perhaps his attack on his office would open some clue to him about what was going to happen to him for the rest of his life. He needed to clear his head.

The college had long suffered from an ongoing cold war over the coffee. McPherson insisted that a pot of coffee required one tablespoon of coffee for each cup. The pot held ten cups; ergo, it needed ten tablespoons. The secretary down the hall, however, cleaned the kitchen and made the initial pot in the morning. She felt that only five tablespoons were necessary. Irascible as McPherson was, he was not prepared to do the clean-up himself, and so the faculty drank weak coffee unless McPherson discovered the pot empty and refilled it. Then they had coffee so strong that people gagged on it.

The red light on the coffee maker shone in the dim light of the kitchen, and the coffee was neither bitter nor dishwater. The evidence argued that he was not alone in the building, and that, moreover, whoever had made it was not an adherent of one of the existing coffee camps. He looked down the other arm of the hallway and saw yellow light spill into the hallway from an open door. Willie's door. Jerry took his coffee and walked down the hallway. Apparently she too was emptying her office. The hallway was filled with cardboard boxes, and he noticed as he approached that a red trolley leaned against the wall.

"Cleaning up?" he asked.

"Cleaning out," she answered. "I'm leaving."

"Going anywhere in particular?"

"I've got a job in Windsor. Good-bye to frozen fingers and giant mosquitoes."

"Can you do that? Can you simply resign and head out in the middle of the year? Don't they make you sign a contract? Hold you in thrall for seven years or something?"

"I was only a sessional. I did have a yearly contract, but they didn't make me stick to it. In this market you've got to grab a job when it's offered or you'll never get one. Didn't you hear about it? You must be the only person on campus who doesn't know I'm leaving."

"That's me," Jerry said. "Always the last to know."

"I'll miss you guys," Willie said. "I liked the college. It was like living in an old British comedy, one of those *Carry On* things with James Robertson Justice. That was him, right? The big guy with the beard who played judges and things?"

Jerry nodded agreement, though he had no idea whether she was right or not. He had always hated those films. "So this is it?"

"Game over. I'm outta here. I'm history. And not a second too soon."

"I'll miss you."

"I'll miss you, too. And Edgar. I'm really going to miss Edgar. The one voice of sanity in this place."

"Edgar is mad as a hatter."

"True. But it's hard to tell. You really have to pay attention."

"Is he back? Is he taking his medication?"

"No. He says he's never coming back. He's on permanent disability."

"What about Elena? What's she going to do?"

"Elena has had a rough spot lately, but she'll be fine. She's actually a really nice person when you get to know her. You should make an effort."

"Thanks no. You're probably right. Almost everybody is a nice person if you get to know them. Probably even the Dean is a nice person, but life is too short to find out how nice everybody is. I think it's important to treasure your enemies. A good enemy is hard to find. Some people go through their whole lives without an enemy. Think about that."

Willie seemed to be thinking about it, but she came over

to him instead and gave him an unexpected kiss on the cheek.

"There," she said. "Now we're even. And you really are sweet. Too bad you didn't follow through. Now we'll never know."

"Yes," Jerry answered. "That's what the golf pro said. It's my follow-through. I never follow through and I end up slicing into the rough. I've spent most of my life trying to get out of the rough."

"Try your mashie-niblick."

"Yes, I suppose that's the answer. I'll just have to get to work on my mashie-niblick."

BACK AT HIS OFFICE, Jerry concluded that Willie was wrong. He was not sweet. Whatever could be said about him, he was not sweet. And once again he had failed to follow through. She had implied that if he had pursued her with more diligence something might have happened. But had he actually wanted anything to happen? The counsellor had been right. He really did need to figure out what it was that he wanted.

The first message was from Shelley. She sounded a little drunk, and he supposed that the message must have been sent shortly after he had left her partying with the students. He really had been deposed. The Commander had told her that she was to ask him to return all the graduate student files and report to his office the first thing on his return to the university after the break. Jerry lifted the pile of graduate student files from his desk and dropped them into the wastebasket.

The police had come by, Shelley went on. Something about a fire. They wanted to interview him about a barn that had burned down in the countryside. She had defended him,

Shelley said. She had told them that he didn't go around burning up barns. They had asked for his phone number and address, but she had given them the wrong address. She had given them the Dean's home phone and address. She appeared to think this was terribly funny, and she burst into giggles. She did not hang up, and Jerry could hear male laughter in the background until finally the machine cut her off.

All Jerry needed now was to spend Christmas in jail. He had not burned down the barn, though he had watched it burn. What was the survivalist's name? Maguire? Would Maguire vouch for him? And if he did, what would his word be worth?

Before he could consider the ramifications of his future as a criminal, Evelyn's voice scratched into the early morning air. She was just phoning to thank him for being a good friend, and she hoped that he would not worry too much about her death. It was too bad that things had gone wrong. They might have put together a decent few years. It didn't matter now. She had cancer and was going to die anyway. She might as well put off the agony of waiting. There was a second of near silence when she might have been weeping, then a decisive click.

Evelyn had not committed suicide, Jerry was certain. It was one more ploy to make him feel guilty. But maybe that was his own justification. Maybe she had killed herself and had died thinking that he was responsible for her death. And maybe he was. Maybe his own callous selfishness had made him blind to her virtues. What had she ever done other than desire him? What were her faults? Her lack of beauty was not a moral failure, and he hadn't been winning any beauty contests himself.

Before he could balance sins of omission with Willie and sins of commission in respect to Evelyn, his mother's voice subsumed all of his guilt into a single weapon and delivered it to him. He had forgotten his sister at the airport. They had taken a cab to the hotel and spent the night there. They were coming over for lunch, and he had better be there, or he was going to be written out of the family. Even Hubert thought he was an ungrateful son, and Hubert used to like him.

Jerry groaned audibly. It was already eleven o'clock. He'd have to leave immediately to get a bus home, then pick up his car and get to his mother's house. It was impossible. He would have to take a cab.

The final voice was Colby's. Jerry got the first part of the message he had missed. Colby had the ideal job for him. He could edit an Australian tourist magazine that Colby had just bought. Jerry would be ideal for the job, since he would be a tourist himself and would know what tourists wanted. Then he went on to the weather.

Jerry phoned the airport. There were no tickets available unless he wanted to go first class and even then there was only one place available, Boxing Day at noon. The price astounded him, but he booked it anyway. He bought lottery tickets. Somewhere, below the level of conscious thought, he believed in an afterlife. Why shouldn't he buy a ticket to Australia? Then he called a cab and went down to the front door to wait for it.

His sister, Carol, opened the door to his mother's house. She looked younger than he had expected, younger, certainly, than she looked on the Christmas card with the picture of the happy family that had been the main source of their communication for nearly twenty years. She was trim and dark, dressed in jeans and a tee-shirt, so that she looked very much like the teenager he remembered.

"The police were here," were her first words.

"And they've taken Mother off to the penitentiary?" Jerry added. "Break and enter, kidnapping, holding a hostage against his will."

"They were looking for you. The Hubert thing has been solved for a long time. Hubert phoned the nursing home and apologized for not giving notice. No, they seem to believe that you may have information about a fire on a farm, and they left a number for you to phone."

"I saw a fire in an old barn. I'd gone to a meeting there, and the fire started accidentally. I did not set it, and I have no information that they could not have got from a dozen other sources."

"What kind of meetings do you go to in old barns?"

"It's a long story with many turnings, and you don't want to hear it. Trust me."

Just then his mother came into the kitchen where they were standing.

"Oh, it's you," his mother said, with the usual note of disappointment in her voice, as if she had been expecting someone else, someone much more interesting and attractive.

"How's Hubert?" Jerry asked.

"He has the flu. He's probably going to die."

"He probably won't die from the flu, Mother," Carol said. She had been away too long, Jerry reflected, and she hadn't yet caught on to her mother's tricks.

"It usually kills old men. That's why they call it the old man's friend."

"That's pneumonia," Jerry said. "He doesn't have pneumonia."

"You're not a doctor. You don't know that."

"Hubert will be fine."

Hubert himself shuffled into the room. He had become incredibly thin since Jerry had last seen him. He was wearing sheepskin slippers, and he didn't raise his feet from the floor as he walked. He very nearly tripped over the throw rug in front of the sink, where he had gone to get a glass of water. Perhaps Jerry had reassured his mother too quickly. Hubert looked as if he could lie down in a coffin and imitate a corpse without even adjusting his expression.

"Are we ready?" he asked. "Are we going right away?"

"No, Hubie," his mother said. "Let's go back and lie down. You need your rest." She led the matchstick-thin Hubert back into the living room, pausing only to say, "Have you told him yet?" in a stage whisper that was much louder than her usual voice.

"No, Mother," Carol said. "I'll tell him in a minute."

"Tell him what?"

"About the house," Carol said. "We've been talking."

"Yes, of course. What else would you do?"

"No. About the house. This is a bit uncomfortable. Would you like a cup of coffee?"

"No. I'm trying to cut down. And nothing you could tell me about the house could be as uncomfortable as the house itself. So carry on. The house."

"Well, Mother and Hubert have decided to move into a senior citizens' home. Bob and I are going to buy the house and fix it up. It needs a lot of fixing."

"It certainly does. But will the senior citizens' home accept them? They are living in sin, you know. The senior citizens' homes tend to operate on a nineteen-forties moral code."

"They are getting married next Wednesday. The Justice of the Peace is coming to the house."

"If Hubert survives that long. He looks as if he had already come back from the dead. Are you sure it was a nursing home she found him in and not a charnel house?"

"The thing is, she has offered to give us the house. It's not really worth very much, and it needs a lot of work, and frankly, it's not an area that we really want to live in. I don't know if you've noticed that it has run down a lot of late."

"Actually, I thought it had improved. Lots of colourful new immigrants, children and laughter in the streets, exciting new produce in the grocery stores. It's a great new area."

"You know what I mean. The thing is, though, that you have a claim on the house. You stand to inherit half of it."

"It's her house," Jerry said. "She can do what she wants with it."

"I don't want to steal anything that is rightfully yours."

"I don't want this house," Jerry said. "It's ridden with ghosts and horrible memories of my un-misspent youth. Failed hours spent studying geometry when I could have been out drinking and doing the act of darkness with the neighbourhood lasses."

"Be serious."

"I am serious. But if you're feeling guilty, I'll make you a deal. You keep the house along with outbuildings and all contents and chattels. I will relinquish all claim. In return, when Hubert dies next Thursday, Mother is your problem. I don't want to see her walking down Main Street with all her belongings in a shopping cart."

"You don't need to make any deal," Carol said. "Of course, I will take care of Mother."

"Then it's a deal," Jerry said, thrusting out his hand so that she had little choice but to shake it.

"You're sure?"

"Absolutely."

Jerry waited only as long as served the needs of decency. He did not wish to do anything that might lead Carol to change her mind. They caught up in a desultory way with the details of family life that could be told to strangers, but Carol could think of little beyond what repairs the house needed, and how it might be remodelled, and Jerry feared that he might say something that would break the charm and return his mother and her decaying house to his care. They were both in excellent moods when they parted, so much so that Jerry forgot that he didn't have his car, and when he couldn't find it, worried at first that it had been stolen. When he remembered that he had left it at home, he was faced with the problem of going back into the house. Instead, he walked down to the little grocery store at the corner, and called a cab from there.

JERRY'S EUPHORIA EVAPORATED on the taxi ride home. Evelyn was either dead or mad, but either way, he was going to have to confront her, and he did not look forward to that. The meeting with the Commander was going to loom over him, however much he realized that nothing would come of it. The Commander had a trick of setting up mysterious meetings with the implication that they would be trials that you would have to face, but knowing the Commander's devices did nothing to eliminate Jerry's anxiety.

And then there was the police. Was it possible that he could in some way be held responsible for the fire? He was the first to notice it, and perhaps Pyncheon and his crew thought that he had set it. Why else would the police want to speak to him?

And over it all loomed the inevitable Christmas party. Thelma was back and settled in his bed. What kind of madness had led him to agree to that? He longed for the days when Elena and Thelma had stalked him in the hallways of the university, when his only concerns were Rover and his assaults on the neighbourhood flower beds and the empty cage where late the sweet bird sang.

And he had better cancel the ticket while he could still get his money back. His flight was scheduled for Boxing Day at noon. It was now four o'clock on Christmas Eve. If he didn't cancel it right away, all the offices would be closed, and he would have to pay the cost of a ticket to Australia for the sake of a momentary fantasy.

The taxi pulled up at Jerry's house. He paid the driver and got into his own car and started it. He could drive to a hotel, register under a false name, and stay there until all his daughters went home. There would still be the problem of getting Thelma out of the house, but he could solve that later. Or he could face up to life, walk into the house and face the music.

He got out of the car and walked up to the door. At each step, he had the option of turning back, but he forced himself, one step at a time, to walk to the door and turn the key in the latch. The key didn't turn.

Not that it mattered. The door was opened almost immediately by Leon, who was looking almost ghostly. Pete, seated at the table, was making marks on paper with a pen. The table was covered with sheets of paper and brochures with pictures of airplanes on them.

"Doing your homework?" Jerry asked.

"Making a business plan," Leon confessed, as if they had been caught with the plans for robbing a bank. "Pete and I are considering a little business venture."

Jerry sensed that their business venture was somehow going to involve him, and he tried to deflect the conversation as quickly as he could.

"Where are the women?" he asked. If he could get his daughters around him, he might put off the conversation about the business plan for as long as he could.

"Margaret is out for a drink with someone named Debbie. Thelma is visiting a friend, and Lise and Cindy have taken the dog to the vet. Apparently it isn't responding to the medication. It pissed all over the floor and is drinking water as if it were going out of style."

"That's Rover," Jerry said. "A thousand little endearing tricks. Where did Margaret go for her drink?"

Pete couldn't remember. Leon thought it might have been a place called Lombardo's. It was near the university, anyway, because Thelma had dropped her off, and they had discussed the fact that it was near the university. Not Lombardo's, Jerry realized. Leonardo's. It was a small restaurant with a bar between Wendy's and The Carpet Factory. Nobody from the university ever went there, and Jerry had never been there himself.

"Anyway," Jerry went on, "I'm sorry about last night. I haven't been drinking much lately, and that Scotch went right to my head. I don't actually remember what I said, but I know I was probably offensive. Too much Scotch always does that to me."

"No, no," both Leon and Pete protested. They had not noticed. He had behaved himself. Everybody had said more than they meant. He should just forget about it.

"There's something we would like your advice on," Pete said. "Leon and me have got this business plan."

Jerry knew he was trapped. He was going to have to approve of some plan that his daughters were going to hate. It was going to be the men against the women. Leon and Pete had the false impression that his approval would have some effect on his daughters. There was not much he could do but listen, and then weasel his way out of making any comment on the plan's viability. Or, better still, he might approve immediately, get out of the way, and watch the boys take their lumps.

Pete began. "There's a fortune to be made in crop spraying. Very few people do it, and those who do usually run marginal equipment and fly-by-night operations. We think that if we could professionalize the operation, we could make a killing."

Leon went on. "There's only about a one-month season, so the people who do it are usually failed farmers who like to fly their own planes but aren't working in the spraying season. They are amateurs. They have to make their entire year's salary in one month, and so they have to charge too much. And if anything happens to their planes, they lose the whole season before they can get them repaired."

"Here's the terrific part," Pete said. "Leon has connections with a flying school. If we could buy two planes, we could handle all the business we could get for the spraying season, and rent the planes to the flying school for the rest of the year."

Jerry could see the problem right away.

"And you guys would pilot the planes yourselves?"

"Exactly."

"And you are not exactly getting encouragement from your women? They've read the articles that say that the average lifespan of a crop sprayer is thirty-two minutes, about the same as a fighter pilot in the Vietnamese war?"

"Only because most guys have terrible equipment, and most of them don't know how to fly," Pete told him.

"Unlike you?"

"Pete is going to learn to fly properly," Leon said. "It will be safer than driving a car."

"Well," Jerry said, "lots of luck selling it to the women. I'm going to miss seeing you guys around."

"The women will be fine," Pete said. "We've already talked to them. They were a little reluctant at first, but they'll come around."

"The thing we're concerned about is financing," Leon said. "We've got to raise about seven hundred and fifty thou. Even with the ranch and my airplane, we're a little short of security. We were wondering whether you'd be prepared to sign a loan for us."

"It's an absolutely safe deal," Pete went on. "The flying school will more than cover the payments on the loan."

Jerry wished he were anyplace else on earth. Very probably, their plan would work. But if it didn't, he would be an indentured servant for the rest of his days. He thought of Thompson in Economics, who had financed his daughter and her husband in a Greek restaurant they had started, and was still teaching at the age of eighty-three to pay off the bankruptcy. He was a walking reminder to the entire faculty of the need for financial conservatism. And he was in Economics, so should have had some idea about what he was letting himself in for.

"I have to think," Jerry said. "It's a big commitment, and I have to have some time to think about it."

"It's a sure winner," Leon said. "And as a silent partner, you stand to make a bundle."

Jerry's head swam. He couldn't concentrate on what was being said. He had no money, no security, nothing to offer. He had the house, they reminded him. That would be all they needed. They had already talked to the banker. Thelma had already signed. They put the paper in front of him.

Jerry hesitated. "Only if you take Rover. Only if you promise to clean up all the shit he deposits in the neighbour's yard."

They promised.

Jerry signed.

"Thelma had the locks changed," Jerry said rather than asked.

"Yes. She said that if she was going to be living here, she

had to have access to the house." Leon was folding up the papers and putting them into a leather briefcase.

"She couldn't ask for another key?"

"She asked for a key last night, remember? You said she could have a key when hell froze over."

"How did she get a locksmith on Christmas Eve?"

Leon and Pete looked at each other. Jerry needed no further confirmation about who the suspects might be. Probably, that was the cost of Thelma's signing. The air in the room was so thick with the ambience of conspiracy that Jerry felt he had to get out of there.

"I've just remembered I left my marking at the university. I better go get it."

"You're going to mark on Christmas day?"

"That's the life of the professor," Jerry said. "There is never release from marking." And he fled from the house, out into the evening, where it was dark and snow was falling even though it was only five o'clock.

"Don't be long," Pete advised. "The girls have something special planned for this evening."

"Don't worry about me," Jerry said. "I'll be fine."

Jerry had no idea where he was going, but the car, like a faithful horse, took him toward the university. He was already past Leonardo's when he realized that he was going there. He had no idea what he intended to do when he got there, but he seemed on a mission that had its own direction.

Jerry pulled into the parking lot and found a spot near the door. The radio warned that a blizzard was on its way from Colorado. There was a chance that it might slip by to the north, but drivers were warned that if they left the city, it was likely that all roads would be closed before they could get back. Just what Jerry needed, a storm that would lock him in with his family for three days of conversation. He was certain that he would not be able to stand it, that something inside him would explode. The snow was already deep in the parking lot, and though the wind was still light, the temperature continued to drop.

He met Margaret coming out the door.

"What are you doing here?" he asked.

"I was having a drink with a friend. And what are you doing here? You haven't been home all day, and nobody knew where you were."

"I was visiting your grandmother, and I hope that you'll find the time to visit her yourself." If they were going to play guilt games, Jerry was not without weapons. "Your aunt Carol and her husband Bob and all the little Bobs and Bobettes are spending Christmas with Grandma."

"Oh, well, I will, I'll phone them tonight. And just as a bit of advice, you should probably apologize to Pete and Leon. You were pretty offensive."

"A good offence is the best defense," Jerry told her. "But I have already apologized. I have also offered them their pound of flesh. Bared my chest like the faithful pelican and allowed them to rip out my heart."

"Are you going to be long?" Margaret asked. "Because I could use a ride home."

"I'll probably be quite a while. I'm meeting Anderson. University business."

"University business on Christmas Eve?"

"It's the way we do things here."

"Well, try not to be too long. I'd better go catch my bus or I'll be here for another hour." Margaret walked out into the falling snow.

No sooner had she left the building than Debbie walked out of the washroom. She spotted him at the door.

"Look who's here," she said.

"Yes," Jerry said. "It's me. And you are also here. Can I buy you a drink?"

"Actually, I've just had one. And I'd sooner not start Christmas with a hangover. But I'll have a coffee and sit through one with you if you like."

Jerry looked into the little bar. Everybody there sat on stools at high tables, and the place was crowded, filled with people who had finished work and weren't anxious to go home yet. There was an air of forced gaiety in the room, women laughing too loudly and men being expansive and masterful. The background music was low, but it was undeniably rap music, and Jerry knew that before many minutes he would hate it so much he would have to leave.

"Can we go somewhere else?" he asked. "This is precisely the sort of ambience I can't stand. It depresses me."

"I thought it was sort of happy."

"Well, that's it. I can't stand happiness."

"You could give me a lift home so that I don't have to wait in the cold for a bus. I could offer you a glass of Scotch, but that's all I have. Scotch and a couple of bottles of light beer."

JERRY WORRIED THAT HE MIGHT GET STUCK in the parking lot, but his little car drove easily through the deepening snow, slipping a little as he turned out onto the street. The radio was still on, and the announcer informed them that the blizzard was certainly on its way. Drivers were warned to stay off the highways. The temperatures would rise with the blizzard, but people should not be fooled. It could be deadly to be caught outside.

Debbie lived on the third floor of an ugly green apartment

block. The hallway smelled of garbage and of steaks cooking. The elevator was slow, and a young man of elephantine proportions rode up with them. He had a terrible cold, and the elevator seemed full of disease. He stared at Jerry as if daring him to comment on his size. Jerry read the elevator licence and tried to decipher the name of the government minister who had signed it.

Debbie's apartment was as depressing as the rest of the building. She had an old chesterfield and chair, a small television and a print depicting a knight saving a damsel in distress from a dragon, done in a futuristic style. Through the open door to the bedroom, he could see a blow-up mattress on the floor. Debbie turned on the television and went to the kitchen to mix Jerry his glass of Scotch. The news was on, and the announcer talked about a massive earthquake that had killed hundreds, with thousands missing. Desperate people wailed in the streets, and bulldozers moved away the rubble. The announcer did not say where this had taken place, but Jerry felt it didn't matter. He had seen the images a hundred times before.

Debbie brought Jerry his Scotch, then relented and poured herself the dregs of a bottle of red wine into a small fruit glass. She held it to the light, but it was far too cloudy to give any indication of its quality. Al Green appeared on the television set, looking like a movie star who had passed his prime. He was talking about a small new film company that was engaged in an exciting new feature-film project.

"Is he allowed to do that?" Jerry asked. "Shill for his own company while pretending to be providing objective news?"

"Everybody does that," Debbie said. "There's no such thing as objective reporting."

"Well, there ought to be," Jerry said. "If we can't get truth in a shitty little television station in a shitty little prairie town where there is nothing at stake, how can we get it anywhere?"

"Precisely," Debbie said, as if Jerry had been in agreement with her all along. "You're not getting any truth anywhere."

"But that doesn't have to be," Jerry said. "People can decide to tell the truth, to live the truth. All they have to do is make a decision and stick to it."

"And who is going to do that?"

"Me," Jerry told her. "I am going to do that. I am going to live my life from now on. I am not going to be a casual bystander to my own life, watching it slip away, while I play out somebody else's script."

"Good for you," Debbie said. "How do you propose to start?"

"I've already started," Jerry said. "I've given away all my worldly goods." That, he reflected, was probably true, if his suspicions of Leon and Pete's enterprise were correct. "I have bought a ticket to Australia, and I am leaving immediately."

Now that he had said the words aloud, the act seemed almost accomplished. He could see palm trees in his imagination. A cool ocean breeze flitted through the room. He imagined the distant cry of a kookaburra.

"Great," Debbie said. "Go for it."

"Will you come with me?" he asked. "We could start over completely anew." Now that he had asked the question seriously, everything depended on her answer.

"No," Debbie said. "I've done that too many times, run away to get a new start. All that happens is that you find you have to run away again."

"This would be different," Jerry said. "It would be a whole new world. It wouldn't even be North America."

Debbie looked as if she were considering Jerry's offer, but she said no again. "If there really was any chance that you would go, or if you went, that you would stay, I might consider it. But you know this is only a fantasy. You aren't going anywhere. You've been here for twenty-five years. You actually love your job, whatever you say. And you've decided to try to put your marriage together again. It looks to me like you're staying put."

"How do you know that, about my marriage?"

"I just had a drink with Margaret, remember?"

"And she told you that everything had been magically put right and we're going to live happily ever after?"

"She said that she was cautiously optimistic. Thelma was meeting with Elena today to tell her the news."

Jerry had not expected that. He was not sure what it meant.

"What about you?" he asked. "What are you going to do?"

"Well, I have to find another job," Debbie said. "The company is cutting back. Apparently we are entering a depression. In the meantime, I have to hold body and soul together."

"I could help you. I could give you the money for the rent until you get another job."

"No, I am not going to be your mistress. I am going to make an honest living."

"I didn't mean that."

"Yes, of course you did. You can only live one life at a time, Jerry, and there is no room in your life for me as a real live person. I'm actually pretty hard to live with." She took a deep breath and went on.

"Jocko has asked me to move in with him."

"Jocko is a married man with five children and a reputation as a reckless philanderer. He is an authentic, certified monster. You can't move in with him."

"He's actually a sweet guy. He and his wife have been divorced for over a year. It was a pretty bad marriage that they held together for the sake of the kids. Now the kids have gone, and there was nothing left to sustain the marriage."

"In the last two minutes, you have listed me every single

cliché about relationships that I know. 'A bad marriage.' All marriages are bad marriages, especially in retrospect. 'The sake of the kids.' The kids are more damaged by grotesque marriages than by divorces. 'Nothing to sustain it.' Marriages are not structures held together by guy wires and likely to topple in a high wind. And 'sweet guy,' for Christ's sake. If Jocko Degraves is a sweet guy, then I'm the archangel Michael."

"That's quite an outburst. I'm spending Christmas with Jocko and his mother. Then we're being married by a Justice of the Peace at one o'clock on Boxing Day. We need another witness. Would you like to come?"

"No," Jerry said. "I would not like to come. I'll be getting on a plane to Australia at that very moment."

Jerry finished his Scotch, then got his coat out of the closet and prepared to leave.

"You're sure you won't reconsider and come to Australia?"

Debbie stood by the door, tears in her eyes.

"No, Jerry. You have to get your own life together." Then she kissed him and said goodbye. Jerry reeled out into the stale-breathed hallway, the smell of her perfume still clinging to him. He reeled down the elevator and out into the snow. It was still falling heavily, but the wind had not yet begun. He got into the car and pointed it home, but the car had a mind of its own, and it took him to his parking space at the university instead. He had to get home, he knew that. They were all waiting for him there. But he made his way to his office where the red light of his answering machine blinked reassuringly. Jerry ignored it, spread his coat out on the floor and fell into a fitful sleep, his dreams peopled by his child-hood enemies.

HE AWOKE TO A RATTLING IN THE PIPES as the great heart of the college, a furnace somewhere in the basement of the building, threw off its ancient lethargy and gathered itself to do battle with the blizzard that roared outside. It had long been rumoured that the college had two furnaces, a modern electrical system and an old oil system that would go on only in an emergency, and apparently this was its moment. Almost immediately, the room was filled with warmth, something that Jerry could not remember having happened before.

He was stiff from sleeping on the hard floor. He was hungry. And he was filled with a sense of impending doom. He felt the way condemned men must feel early on the mornings of their final day. He ransacked the kitchen and found one small Japanese orange, a couple of soup crackers and a half bottle of dry sack. He ate the orange and the crackers, washed it all down with a couple of good swigs of the sherry, and felt better.

The washroom smelled foul, but then it always smelled foul. Jerry had credited that to the digestive systems of his college fellows, but since no one had been there for days, it must have been something in the system itself, some flaw in the piping that removed the waste products all right, but recycled the odours for the benefit of the college's inhabitants.

He gathered the bottle of sack and took it back to his office. He put it on his desk beside the bottle he had emptied the night before. The light on the answering machine still blinked red, and Jerry considered whether or not he should answer it. He didn't think he could take any more bad news. But then again, what bad news was still out there waiting for him? What else could happen? Thelma was back in his house, and she had changed the locks. Whatever happened there, he was pretty sure she was not going to leave.

Evelyn, like Schroedinger's cat in the classic physics experiment, was either alive or dead, and would only actually enter one state or the other when he found out. And Debbie was getting married on Boxing Day to the last man on earth he would wish for her, a man even older than him, with a larger pot.

He pressed the button reluctantly. The first two messages were false alarms, the hesitant breathing of someone who lost his nerve at the last moment and decided not to leave a message. The third was Evelyn. She sounded lively, full of health, enjoying herself. She apologized for the last call, and said that she was very much alive, and, though still clearly mortal, intended to go on living for the foreseeable future. She had been to see a psychiatrist, who put her on medication that made a world of difference. She was taking six months of stress leave and did not intend to spend it at the university. Maybe she'd go to Spain. Maybe she'd go to Norway. She hoped they could still be friends. She would phone when she got back.

Jerry took a swig of the sherry. It was warm and good. There were no more messages. His office was cleaner than it had been since the day he had entered it. A small piece of blue paper had a long number written on it, and Jerry remembered that this was the number he was to give at the airport to pick up his ticket. He looked up the airline in the yellow pages and phoned to cancel. A voice told him the office hours, but gave him another number to call in case of emergency. He called that number and was told to hold, a customer service representative would be with him as soon as possible. Forty minutes later, he was still holding, listening to some music that seemed vaguely familiar but had no identifiable melody. He hung up, then in a panic dialled again, and found himself in the same position, only forty minutes further from an answer. He hung up again.

He would have to go back to his home. Back to his wife and his daughters and their husbands. The small euphoria the sherry had provided had started to wane, so he finished the bottle in one long draw and put on his coat and went out into the cold.

It was a blizzard, all right. The wind whipped snow into his face so that he had to turn his head aside as he walked toward his car. The noise was terrific. The snow swirled and seemed to come from every direction at once. The main road appeared to have been ploughed, and the wind had cleared the snow from the parking lot and piled it as high as the windows against the college building. His engine turned over slowly twice, then caught into life. There was only one fairly deep drift of snow between Jerry and the street. He backed up to the very door of the college, then got up as much speed as he could and ploughed into the snowdrift. His car swerved sideways and slowed almost to a stop, but it slid across the top of the snow and he found himself out on the street.

There was no traffic at all. Jerry appeared to be the only person driving in the entire city. Ahead of him, he could see the snowplough that permitted this, and he had to slow to follow it. All the side streets were clogged, and cars were stuck at odd angles near the curb. In the darkness of the day, streetlights had come on, though it was not yet noon. At his house, they would have eaten breakfast and opened their presents. No one would have waited for him. They would know that he could not get home.

The snowplough passed Jerry's street and he had to make an instant decision. His street seemed less clogged than the others. He turned and gunned his engine, hoping he might make it the half block to his house. And he nearly did make it. A couple of doors down from him, the snow rose deep in the middle of the street, so Jerry turned and ploughed as far up the boulevard as he could. The Mazda came to rest with the front high off the ground and the tailpipe touching the street. He was completely hung up. He would have to hire a tow truck after the storm and hope he hadn't ruined the suspension or the steering system.

He got out and walked the hundred feet or so to his house. The snow was blinding, and the wind seemed even more furious than before. He took out his keys, then remembered that the locks had been changed, and he rang the doorbell. There was no answer. After a couple of rings, he turned the knob, and the door opened. The kitchen held the remains of a ranch house breakfast of bacon and eggs and waffles, and he could hear loud Christmas music from the living room. He took a deep breath and walked through the door.

Everyone turned to look at him, and for a moment he had the impression that he had caught them in a snapshot, everyone motionless, every mouth open, all gestures frozen for a second. Then the room broke into a pandemonium of speech. His daughters demanded that he tell them where he had been, and why, of all nights, he had missed last night's supper.

It was the storm, he said. He had gone to his office to get his credit card, which he had forgotten there, and he had got stuck. He couldn't get his car out until he found a shovel, and then the streets were clogged, and he had to wait for a snowplough to come by. Why hadn't he phoned? He had tried, but apparently the phone lines to the college had been blown down.

Jerry wondered why he was creating such a formidable collection of lies, why he didn't simply tell the truth. He had not been there because he didn't want to be, because he had only one life, and it was slipping away, and everything he touched turned to disaster. He could have told them that, then gone to his room and got into bed and stayed there until everybody went away.

But of course he couldn't do that either. The presents had been opened, and the floor was strewn with wrapping paper. The sweaters he had bought were draped over the arms of chairs and piled on the coffee table. Somebody had bought and decorated a Christmas tree, and the needles filled the air with the slight scent of cat urine. The music was too loud, and Margaret turned it down so that it was exactly the same loudness as the conversation in the room.

Pete and Leon had an open bottle of Canadian Club between them, and Pete mixed Jerry a strong glass of rye whiskey and Coke, without ice. He asked them how the business plan was going, and Cindy shot him a steely glare. Apparently, the air had not cleared as quickly as the men had hoped.

"Fine, Jerry," Leon said. "We're going down to the lawyer's to finalize everything."

"We are going to the lawyer's to discuss things," Cindy corrected. "There will be plenty of time for finalizing."

Jerry had a moment of hope. Pete's briefcase was near the door. If he could get everyone out of the room under some guise, perhaps he could get the document he had signed and destroy it before they got to the lawyer's. There would still be the problem of Thelma, but he could solve that later.

Later was not to be, because at that moment, Elena came down the stairs and into the room. Jerry looked at her in amazement. She was in a small black dress with a string of pearls, and for a moment he wasn't sure who she was.

"Hello, Jerry," she said.

Jerry didn't know what to say.

"Thelma?" he asked into the air.

"We've decided to get back together," Thelma said. "I realized after we went to the counsellor that there was no hope for you and me. We would both have to change, and neither of us wants to do that. I'm not blaming you for anything, but I think we all have to accept things as they are."

Jerry wasn't sure what he could be blamed for, but he also knew that if he brought up the topic, blame would be found. There was always enough blame to go around.

"Can we sit down and discuss this reasonably?" Elena said. "I don't think we need to hate each other. I think we can work out a civilized arrangement so everyone is happy."

Happiness seemed an extravagant goal to Jerry, but he was clearly not in control, and if they offered him happiness, he supposed he would have to accept it. He looked around the room in mute appeal, but nobody else seemed to notice what was going on, except Pete, who handed him another glass of whiskey, this time omitting the warm Coke. Jerry finished his first drink, and took a good mouthful of the second.

Thelma handed Jerry a typed page with items numbered from one to twelve. Jerry looked at it and saw it was a list of things he must agree to. The first item was that Thelma would live in the house. Good. He would not have to steal Pete's briefcase after all.

Rover chose that moment to walk into the centre of the room, give one mournful howl, then keel over and die. He fell to the floor, so clearly dead that no one even thought of trying to revive him. Every one of Jerry's daughters burst into tears at the same moment. Thelma and Elena seemed equally upset and the room was pandemonium. At the last moment, Rover, like the bird before him, had shat his last, and the smell was overpowering.

Leon came in from the kitchen and walked over to Jerry.

"There's a couple of cops at the back door," he said. "They say they have a warrant for your arrest."

"Tell them I'll be there in a second."

Jerry saw a set of keys in a leather case with "Wild Rose Country" written on it. They were on a shelf of the bookcase by the front door. He picked them up, slipped out the door, and closed it as quietly as he could. He hoped nobody would notice his going.

The road had been ploughed, and a police car with no one in it was parked on the street. Jerry got into Pete's big black Expedition and found the right key. The truck started with a roar. Jerry backed into the street and headed towards the main highway. Now they could add car theft to his charges. He passed his little Miata, almost completely covered with snow. Then, as he turned onto the main road, he saw the lights of the police car behind him start flashing as the police turned it around to follow him. He stepped on the accelerator, and the big machine purred. There was still no traffic at all, and the storm had, if anything, got worse.

After a few minutes, Jerry relaxed. The police did not seem to be following him. He realized that he was heading back to the university, like an animal trained to head for home as soon as there was any danger. He passed the big new Home Fitness Centre that he had come to think of as the half-way point, and saw, in his rear-view mirror, the blinking lights of the police car, still far in the distance, but gaining on him.

On an impulse, he turned left onto a side street that followed the river to a small park and a golf course. It had not been ploughed, and Jerry had a moment of panic as the big Expedition ploughed into the first snowdrift, but the vehicle was high and in four-wheel drive. It drove through the deep snow as if it were travelling on bare Tarmac, and Jerry knew that the police would not follow him further. He relaxed and turned on the radio. Cowboy music flooded the air, and he turned the radio off again.

Then, as Jerry came to a bend in the road near the cemetery where the park began, the snow thickened and swirled so that he could see nothing. It cleared for a moment, and he saw pure white before him with no indication of where the road lay and the park began. Then the snow whirled again, blinding him with whiteness, and the truck lurched and came to a halt in the ditch. Jerry tried to back up, but the truck spun its wheels whichever direction he tried. He was going nowhere.

He knew that the first rule in emergencies of this kind was to stay with the vehicle, but surely that was for rural areas and the open road. He was in the city, surrounded by houses. As long as he kept moving, he would ultimately bump into someone's house, and surely they would not turn away a man lost in a blizzard. He shut off the truck and put the keys in his pocket. Then he thought better of what he had done and put the keys back in the ignition. Nobody was going to steal it out of that ditch.

It took only a moment for Jerry to regret his decision. The wind whipped so strongly that he could not face it. Tiny sharp ice crystals pained him. It was like being in a sandstorm, only this was snow. He returned to where he thought he had left the truck, but the truck was no longer there. It had vanished into the whiteness. He pushed on, certain that he must soon feel the solid road beneath him, but the snow was so deep that he floundered and fell. His wrists, between the edge of his sleeves and his gloves, were now wet and very cold. For the first time it struck him that he might not survive, that he might have blundered in the direction of the river, and he might collapse from the cold before he found help.

He bumped into something and fell heavily into the snow once more. He got up and felt in the snow for the object he had touched. It was a gravestone. That was some help. At least he knew where he was. He had blundered into the graveyard between the road and the river. The wind dropped for a second and he saw headstones on all sides of him, and a small crypt with a statue of an angel in an indentation in the concrete wall. He took a bead on the tiny building and headed for it. The snow closed in again, but in a couple of minutes he reached the crypt and sheltered beside it in the lee of the wind.

It would be a grotesque irony, he thought, to die here in a graveyard on Christmas night when the rest of the world was snuggling down to turkey dinners and glasses of bad red wine. Perhaps he could huddle here and ride out the storm. It could not go on forever.

Still, it showed no signs of abating. Jerry made himself a little nest in the snow and settled in. After only a few minutes, he was cold and restless again. He tried out his voice. He shouted "Help" into the face of the wind and waited. He shouted again. It was pointless. No one was going to hear him. He was going to die here, alone in the storm. It all seemed horribly unfair. He shouted again, and the sound of his own voice gave him courage.

"Thelma," he shouted. "I hate you, Thelma." He did not hate Thelma, he knew that. He did not even hate Elena, but it felt better to shout out hatred, so he shouted again.

"Go home," he shouted to his daughters. "Take your rotten husbands and get out of my life. I raised you and fed you. Isn't that enough?"

"Go away, Evelyn," he cried. "Get out of my life. I don't care anymore."

"Don't marry him, Debbie," he screamed into the wind. "It's a mistake. There's still time."

"Easy, easy," a voice behind him said. "Go back to your grave. It's only a blizzard. Everything is going to be all right."

Jerry turned. Behind him was a tall figure in a parka with a fur hood pulled so tight that Jerry could not make out a face.

"Take it easy," the voice said again, and the figure took his arm. "Here, I'll help you find your grave."

Jerry recognized the voice now. "Edgar?" he asked. He remembered that Edgar lived somewhere near here. Anderson had said he often saw Edgar walking in the cemetery on his way to work. "Is that you, Edgar? What are you doing here?"

"I'm comforting the dead," Edgar said. "They don't like unsettled weather."

"Can you find the way out of here?" Jerry asked.

"It's Jerry, isn't it?" Edgar asked. "Don't worry, you'll get used to it. When did you die?"

"I'm not dead," Jerry told him. "I'm as alive as you are. Can we go to your place and warm up?"

"If you're not dead, then what are you doing here?"

"I got stuck. My truck is stuck in the ditch. Can you help me?"

"We had good times, back in the old days, Jerry," Edgar said. "I liked you. You were the only one who actually listened to me. You were the only one who had read Heidegger. Nobody else cared about the problem of auto-affection, but you did. You worried about the question of agency, about the nature of the subject."

"Yes, I did," Jerry said, trying to reassure Edgar and bring him back to the subject at hand. "I still do. Can we go now?"

"In a minute," Edgar said. "Listen."

Jerry listened. He could hear only the whistle of the wind. "What do you hear?" he asked.

"Voices," Edgar said. "Can't you hear them? The voices of the dead, full of fear of this storm. We have to comfort them." Edgar turned and headed out into the storm. Jerry lunged at him and caught his arm, but Edgar twisted away, and danced out into the whirling wind and snow.

"Don't worry," Edgar said, "I'll be back. I have to comfort

the others." His voice mixed with the roaring of the wind, and though he said something else, Jerry couldn't make out his last words.

Jerry knew then that he was going to die. He would not find his way out by himself. Still, while he had any strength left, he had to try. He calculated where he thought the road and the houses might be, and he walked out into the storm. At first, it was very cold, but after a while Jerry realized that he was unbearably hot. He took off his coat, but that was not enough. He took off his shirt as well and felt better, but very, very tired. He needed only to rest for a few minutes, then everything would be all right. He lay down in the snow and rested.

THE HUM OF THE AIRPLANE'S ENGINES soothed Jerry, and he fell in and out of sleep. The stewardess kept bumping into his shoulder with her hip as she rushed down the aisle. Jerry opened his eyes and saw that the movie was over and people were beginning to stir. His fingers were still numb, and his ears had begun to tingle, but he was lucky, he thought. Possibly the luckiest man on earth.

The first part of the trip across the Rockies to Vancouver had been the hardest part. He had been cold the whole way and worried that something serious had happened to him, something he was not going to be able to deny. But he had warmed up in the airport waiting the two hours for the plane to Hawaii. Edgar's shirt was long in the arms, but a little tight around the chest. The old tweed jacket with the leather patches kept him looking professorial, so he had taken it off in Hawaii and put it into the overhead compartment. He thought he would leave it there when he got off the airplane. He had no plans for looking professorial again.

It was still unclear to him how Edgar had found him and how he had hauled him through the storm and into his house. Edgar's wife had accepted his arrival as if Edgar regularly dragged dying men out of the snow and brought them home. She had made him soup and directed him to the shower, and put him to bed in the guest room without question. She had served him hot oatmeal porridge and orange juice for breakfast, and she had driven him to the airport in time for his flight.

The storm had blown itself out with amazing speed. He had awakened to brilliant sunshine and ploughed streets. The Boxing Day crowds at the mall where they had stopped so Jerry could buy some clothes and a suitcase were heavy and intense. All Christmas cheer had ended, and most people seemed intent on bargains or on returning inadequate presents. Jerry could not even remember quite what he had bought. He would find out when he opened the suitcase. That would be his Christmas present. He supposed that there were probably Christmas presents still waiting for him back at the house, socks and cardigans, though he had always hated cardigans and made his feeling known. But he didn't want to think about the house.

He had phoned Colby from Hawaii, and Colby had vowed to meet him at the airport, even though he was supposed to be in Perth that day. He would cancel everything for a week, and they could catch up, maybe do a little fishing or golfing. Relax. Jerry wondered about the tourist magazine that he was supposed to edit. Colby said there would be plenty of time to think about that later.

Jerry tried to work up some enthusiasm about Australia, but, though he told himself that he was starting a new life, his body refused to respond. He felt old and tired. He hurt. He imagined that the magazine would be as dreary as any university course and Colby would be as overbearing and thoughtless as he had always been. The trip was certain to be a disaster. All that remained was to find out how disastrous it would be.

He ate the meal that was supposed to be a combination of breakfast and lunch, and he stood in the line with the others to use the tiny washroom. When he was settled back in his seat, they began their descent. A few minutes later the airplane bumped twice and landed.

Jerry was the first person off the airplane. Nobody else in first class seemed in any hurry to exit, and he made his leisurely way to the doorway where the steward held back the masses until the privileged few had departed. He was waved through passport control and waited for his luggage. The room had no windows, and though it was large, it seemed dark and gloomy, as if it were about to rain.

Jerry watched the bags dropping down onto the conveyor belt, looking for his new suitcase. He had always thought that if you were in first class, your bags would be the first out. But he had been so late getting to the airport that everyone else was already on board, and so of course his luggage would have been loaded last. He tried to imagine how his bag would have been shuffled from front to back during the various plane changes, but he lost track and it wasn't worth figuring out anyway.

He glanced across the conveyor belt to the people gathered on the other side. The woman directly across from him looked a lot like Debbie. In fact, it was Debbie. She looked at him and smiled, and Jerry's heart nearly burst. He leaped onto the conveyor belt, jumped over the central section, seized her in his arms and kissed her intemperately. He held her tight, and she bit him on the shoulder.

"Ouch," he said. "What was that for?"

"Take it easy," Debbie said. "We've got lots of time."

"But how?" Jerry asked. "What happened to Jocko?"

"He and his mother are entertaining the Justice of the Peace, I guess. After you left that night, Jocko came by and told me all about his plans for what would happen after our marriage. Then I had a horrible Christmas with him and his mother. You were right. He is a monster."

"But how did you get here?"

"I came on the same airplane that you were on, only I was in steerage."

Jerry's bag floated by and he grabbed it from the conveyor belt. Debbie's bag was right beside it. Together, they made their way through customs and out into the waiting room. People held out signs with the names of lost relatives on them, and others flung themselves into waiting arms. There was no one waiting for them. They made their way out into the blazing Australian sun and the ferocious noontime heat. Palm trees waved their fronds, and a kookaburra cried in the distance. Surf crashed on the nearby beaches. Colby was waiting by a large white convertible, and he waved his hat at them. There were probably kangaroos somewhere around but Jerry didn't notice. He had stopped to kiss Debbie again, and the storm that had been raging in his heart had finally blown itself out.